CHRISTOPHER COOL

Ace of Shadows

WHEN enemy agents try to snatch the secret files of Count Dietrich von Kronstein—who has helped refugees escape from behind the Iron Curtain to the West—the count seeks TEEN's help. The U.S. intelligence agency dispatches its two most skilled agents, Chris Cool and his Apache pal Geronimo Johnson, to the count's castle in Bavaria. They arrive in time to witness his funeral! During the services a blowgun dart narrowly misses Chris, but kills a diplomat from the Arab country of Marak.

What happens next catapults Chris and Geronimo into a terrifying race to Marak to East Berlin and back to Bavaria, to prevent an international bargain which could destroy the free world.

The TEEN agents match wits not only with the deadly espionage organization TOAD, but also with the elusive and feared Red spy known as the Ace of Shadows.

**TEEN
Agent** | **CHRISTOPHER COOL**

TEEN
Agent

CHRISTOPHER COOL

Ace

of

Shadows

by JACK LANCER

GROSSET & DUNLAP
PUBLISHERS   NEW YORK

Contents

Ace
of
Shadows

1 · Death at a Requiem

A PROCESSION OF mourners filed slowly past the bier in the dimly lighted chapel of Kronstein Castle. From all over the world people had come to Germany to pay their respects to Count Dietrich von Kronstein.

Among them were Christopher Cool, a lean, blond college sophomore and his Apache roommate Geronimo Johnson, both U.S. TEEN agents. They stopped at the half-opened bronze and silver casket, in which the white-haired count reposed.

"A true aristocrat," Chris whispered.

As they moved on, Geronimo looked faintly puzzled. "Promise her anything, but give her Arpege."

"Can't you ever be serious, Gerry? A TV commercial—"

"I am. Don't you smell it?"

Suddenly Chris realized what his friend meant. A faint scent of strictly feminine perfume hung in the air. But there was no woman in sight.

"Who do you think is wearing it?" Chris asked.

"Brilliant as I am, I can't tell you that."

Several mourners glanced in their direction. Chris, a linguistic genius who could speak fluent Apache among other languages, switched to Geronimo's native tongue. The youths often conversed in that language when they did not want to be understood.

"Notice anything else?"

"No."

"Why the long face?"

"It bugs me, *choonday*, old buddy. I have a hunch we'd better make the scene fast. If someone else gets the count's records ahead of us, there'll be a lot more dead bodies."

"I know. Let's sit down."

A clergyman appeared and took his place in front of the casket. Quiet spread over the room like a thick blanket. The eulogy was short. Graf von Kronstein would be remembered always for his acts of goodness.

Six pallbearers in dark suits raised the coffin and bore it out through the door, where an ornate, glass-enclosed hearse was waiting to carry it to the family mausoleum.

"I still don't believe his death was accidental," Chris muttered.

"Neither do I," Geronimo said.

They rose with the others in the front pews to follow the coffin.

"*Iltse!*" Geronimo shouted suddenly.

At his warning cry of "Watch it," Chris dropped to the stone floor. Something whizzed over his head. A man standing in front of him screamed, arched his back, staggered a few steps, and collapsed.

The TEEN agents rushed to his aid. "No pulse," Geronimo said. "He's dead."

"Look at this!" Chris pointed to a thin red object projecting from the man's back. "A dart! Either from a blowgun or a pneumatic weapon."

"An air pistol. I saw somebody raise it."

"Who?"

"Didn't see his face. I ducked, too." Geronimo looked again at the man before him. "He's been poisoned. Poor fellow was gone before he hit the floor."

A swarthy man with a pugnacious face appeared above them. "This is outrageous! Someone will pay for this. I swear that by the name of Allah!"

Chris looked up in surprise. "You knew this man?"

"Of course. He is the head of the Maraki Consulate—the most esteemed El Sidi."

"He *was*," Geronimo corrected tonelessly.

By orders of Lothar von Kronstein, son of the deceased count, a number of burly peasants stationed themselves at the chapel doors to prevent anyone from leaving. Soon the local police arrived. They frisked the guests, interrogated everyone, and checked foreign passports.

"Got an idea," Geronimo whispered in Chris's ear. "Watch this!"

The two stood close to Count Lothar. The Apache raised his voice in indignation at being held for questioning. "This is preposterous!" he said and turned to Lothar von Kronstein. "You allow such insults to happen to foreign students? Especially Americans?"

Embarrassed, the count tried to interfere, but the police politely but firmly went on with their investigation. Geronimo ranted on. He questioned German hospitality and manners, until Lothar finally disappeared.

The TEEN agents were interrogated and released, with Geronimo still shaking his fist and threatening to bring the wrath of the Apache nation down on the village of Kronstein.

Outside, Chris mopped his brow. "Okay, fearless chief. What was that all about?"

Geronimo grinned sardonically. "I should get an Oscar for a fine performance."

"Agreed, but why?"

"To get an invitation to Kronstein Castle."

"No kidding."

"Don't you see? The count is pretty embarrassed, and foreign students like us with a lot of connections in Munich can easily spread the word that he's a fink."

"Think it'll work?"

"If it doesn't, I'll feel like a bigger fool than Custer."

Chris and Geronimo were members of TEEN, the Top-secret Educational Espionage Network. It was a hush-hush and highly effective corps of brilliant young spies developed by the CIA under the direction of an espionage genius known only as Q.

Only the day before yesterday the two had been pursuing their studies at Kingston University, when they were suddenly summoned to headquarters in New York City.

Q, in his usual navy-blue blazer, wore one of his infrequent smiles. "Know anything about etiquette in German aristocratic circles, Cool?" he asked, handing Chris a decoded note. It read:

REQUEST TRANSFER MY FILES ON POLITICAL REFUGEES TO UNITED STATES. SUSPICIOUS ONE OF MY GUESTS JESSICA VALORSKY IS ENEMY AGENT TRYING TO OBTAIN RECORDS. IMMEDIATE ANSWER APPRECIATED. COUNT DIETRICH VON KRONSTEIN

The count, explained Q, possessed a wealth of detailed records concerning refugees who, with his help, had slipped through the Iron Curtain to the West. The documents included intelligence on escape networks and other pertinent data.

"And we're supposed to see the count and handle the transfer?" Chris asked.

"Eh, not exactly." Q cleared his throat and handed Chris another note. "This came from Munich two hours ago." The TEEN agent read:

VON KRONSTEIN KILLED IN ACCIDENTAL FALL. PAPERS WHEREABOUTS UNKNOWN. JESSICA VA-LORSKY MISSING. REQUEST ASSISTANCE IMMEDI-ATELY.

"He's dead!" Chris exclaimed.

"Quite so. You are registered at the University of Munich as exchange students and will leave at once. No time for briefing. That'll be done by our Munich contact."

Twelve hours later Chris and Geronimo touched down at the Munich airport aboard a commercial jetliner. They took a limousine into the city and checked in with their contact, a man named Sepp who ran a cheese-and-sausage shop.

Sepp had a black Porsche waiting. The boys drove through the sunny Bavarian countryside to the village of Kronstein, took a room at the inn, and attended the funeral.

Now back at the inn, they waited for Lothar's reaction. It came an hour later by special messenger. A handwritten note asked the boys to accept his Teutonic hospitality and spend a few days as his guests at the Schloss.

"Your war dance did it, Gerry!" Chris grinned. "We're in!"

He phoned their acceptance immediately and apologized for the behavior of his friend, explaining that Geronimo had not been feeling well lately. This, plus his excitable Apache blood, had been responsible for his outburst.

It was quite late and mist swirled around the car as the boys drove up the long, winding road to Schloss Kronstein, located on top of a hill overlooking the village. The narrow road, forested on both sides by towering black pines, opened onto a cobblestoned courtyard. On one side, a low stone fence knifed along a dizzying precipice. One hundred yards opposite the barrier stood a forbidding iron gate.

When Chris turned off his headlights, a uniformed guard stepped out, checked their credentials, and let them inside.

Judging from the few lights glowing in the windows of the castle, nearly everyone had retired. The TEEN agents were greeted by a butler and shown to their room.

"Breakfast will be at nine in the Gold Room," he told them and left.

They lay down on their huge, twin four-poster beds and waited half an hour in silence.

"Ready?" Chris said finally.

Geronimo nodded.

Chris checked the hallway before they stepped out. Sepp had told them where to find Jessica Valorsky's room. It was at the head of the stairs.

Chris took a pen from his sports coat, plucked off the cap, and eased the door open a few inches. He held the pen to his eye. If the room was occupied, the snooperscope would reveal the person in ghostly red outline. "Empty," Chris stated.

The youths entered quickly, closed the door, and began a quick but methodical search with miniature pocket flashlights.

An hour later they had found nothing. "Someone cleaned out every trace of Jessica," Chris said and added, "One more time. Then we'll call it a night."

"Pay dirt!" Geronimo whispered a few moments later. "Stuck to the underside of the throw rug."

It was a scrap of paper. The name *El Sidi* was scrawled upon it and check-marked.

"Looks as if we were right," Chris said. "That dart *was* meant for El Sidi and not me. But how is the assassination of a Maraki diplomat tied in with this case?"

Geronimo shrugged.

They finished their search and went back to their room, where they changed into their pajamas in the dark. Chris stood with one foot propped on the window sill. He stared down through the mist rising over a large lake, which he had not seen on the ride up. The water's edge met an open field, which gave way to a park nestled at the base of the turreted castle. Finally Chris's eyes came to rest on the dark, strange-shaped shadows of trees and shrubbery below.

A Maraki official, an enemy agent, a German count, missing records. What was the connection?

A bright light blinked in the mist.

"Gerry! There's someone down there."

Geronimo squinted. "Can't make him out. Looks like a big man in a cloak and a wide-brimmed hat."

"The tower, Gerry! Someone's answering him with another light. Recognize the code?"

"It's Greek to me."

"Not Greek, buddy. I'd have it in three seconds flat if it were."

Chris pulled out the stem of his wrist-watch transceiver and set it to Transmit. "Keep an eye on those lights, Gerry. I'll contact Sepp."

He spoke into the radio. "Wunny Kingston to Uncle Seymour. Come in, please."

There were a few seconds of silence, then "Uncle Seymour here. *Was gibts, Probleme?*"

"No problem, but some interesting developments. We have one on the line now." Chris described the lights and the cloaked figure. "Just before, we—"

"Watch out!" Sepp warned. "You may be up against the Ace of Shadows!"

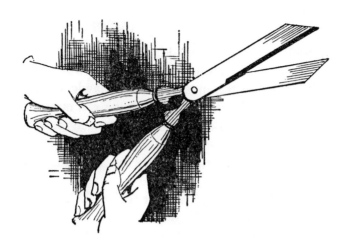

2 · White Lie

"The Ace of Shadows?" Chris repeated.

"*Ja*. He is a Red agent. Most feared and deadly. An expert on southeast Europe. No one has ever really seen him, only his shadow."

"*Choonday*," Geronimo said, "the lights are out. I can't figure why, but our Dracula-type friend is still there. Hasn't budged an inch."

Chris related the information to Sepp.

"Strange," their contact said. "But then the man is an enigma. More than once agents have complained, 'How does one catch a shadow?' Be cautious."

"Don't worry."

"*Gut*. I have additional information about Fräulein Valorsky. She is not from the other side.

Actually she's from *no* side. She's from TOAD."

"Great!" Chris said sarcastically.

TOAD was the most lethal and lawless secret organization in the world. A huge criminal set-up, it was working piece by piece toward eventual world domination. Its intelligence network at times outshone even the Russian KGB and the CIA.

"I don't scan that," Chris continued. "How do they figure in this?"

"We have no answers yet. But be advised that Fräulein Valorsky is a master of disguise." Sepp gave Chris the best available description of the woman.

"Any more monkey wrenches to toss at us?" Chris asked.

Sepp chuckled. "*Nein.* That is enough for now, I believe. *Gute Nacht.*"

"*Auf Wiedersehen.*"

Chris went to the window, where Geronimo still eyed the mysterious figure.

"Pony soldier, that cat down there hasn't moved in half an hour. If he's been paralyzed, he'll be there in the morning. If he splits, we'd lose him in the fog anyway. So let's hit the sack, huh?"

"Agreed," Chris replied.

There were several guests at the Schloss and next morning Chris and Geronimo saw Count Lothar only briefly. He was a slender man in his early thirties, slightly above average height. He bore hints of his father's aristocratic features, but Lothar's face seemed to be blunted by an indefinable coarseness.

"I am glad you accepted my invitation," the count said to Geronimo in English that was nearly free of accent. "Please make yourselves at home here." He excused himself to greet another guest.

After breakfast the TEEN agents went to investigate the area from which the signals had come the night before. The place proved to be a small park of thick hedges and trees.

"Dig those crazy vegetables," Geronimo said. "Whoever dreamed up those shapes must be one wild medicine man."

"It's topiary," Chris said.

"White man's magic?"

"The art of trimming and training trees or shrubs into odd or ornamental shapes."

"I thought it was limited to representational sculpture—you know, birds, animals, and the like."

"Not necessarily. I think the dead count had taste."

The forms were abstract and free, just suggestive enough to fire the imagination.

"Hey, *choonday*! I guess I've found the Ace of Shadows!"

Chris whirled. *"What!"*

"Here he is." Geronimo was standing next to a tall bush. From a long central cylinder, the leaves flared out into a kind of mantle. "Viewing it from our room, you might see the outline of a man in a cape. That tree branch behind it would serve as the hat."

Chris stroked his chin. "I think you're right. I wonder if it was arranged that way on purpose."

Geronimo shrugged. "In any case, someone *was* out here signaling."

They examined the immediate area. "Hey, take a look at this!" Geronimo picked up a lace handkerchief snagged on a thorny bush. "J.V.," he said, reading the initials. "Jessica Valorsky."

Chris grinned. "That figures. Girls are always losing something." He sniffed the perfumed handkerchief. "Expensive stuff. *Petit Mensonge.* 'White Lie.'"

"Let me smell it." Geronimo inhaled the musky odor. "That's the same scent I smelled at the funeral! Our girl Jessica was there, probably in disguise. She might have put the dart into El Sidi!"

Before Chris could reply, they were interrupted by a wizened man with reddish hair and a rust-colored beard who stepped from behind a hedge. Frowning and unfriendly, he was dressed in soiled work clothes and held a pair of pruning shears in his hand. *"Was machen Sie hier?"* he demanded.

"We're admiring the topiary," Chris said genially. "Are you the gardener?"

"*Ja.* Drucker's the name."

"Your handiwork is . . . is . . ." Chris faked ignorance of the language. "Is very *nett.*"

The gardener's expression did not change. He muttered something in German. Chris smiled blankly and the boys walked away.

Out of earshot, Geronimo asked, "What did he say? I didn't get it."

"Things won't be the same, whatever that means."

"Good man to have on a scalping party. What next—the tower?"

"Yes." They walked out of the park toward the thick base of the soaring tower that buttressed the north end of the castle at the lake's edge. It took both of them to pull open the huge, oak-over-iron door. The rusty hinges creaked. In gloom, they began climbing the spiral stone stairway.

"Halloo," called a voice behind them. "Wait, please." Footsteps clambered up. It was Lothar.

"I saw you enter the tower, but I was too far away to warn you. Please. It is not safe here. Age has weakened the structure. The possibility of collapse exists. The door should have been locked."

"Sorry," Chris said. "We didn't know. We'll cross it off our sight-seeing list."

"I would be grateful."

They descended the stairs with the count. Two business associates were waiting for Lothar at the ground level and he walked off with them.

"Smell fishy, *choonday?*" Geronimo asked.

"Like a whale, but we'll have to put it off."

They decided that Chris would scout the rest of the castle while Geronimo drove into the village to see what he could pick up from the grapevine. The Apache took the Porsche, gunning the engine and zooming out of the driveway with a spray of gravel. The winding road was deserted, except for a farm boy sitting under a tree listening to a small radio.

Less than a kilometer from the village, a man staggered out of the woods and collapsed. The Indian braked to a squealing halt, leaped from the car, and rushed to help. At the same instant, two figures charged from cover and the fallen man jumped to his feet. They closed in on the TEEN agent.

"*Ai,*" Geronimo thought. "The innocent farm boy must have been a spy."

Yelling an Apache war cry, he caught his first attacker on the chin with a savate kick. He locked the second man in a wristhold and used his shoulder to send him flying. The third man knew hand-to-hand combat and immediately assumed a classic karate defensive position. Geronimo circled warily, saw an opening, and attacked. The hard edge of his hand smashed into the side of the man's neck.

The fellow gasped, reeled, then countered with a stiff-fingered drive to the solar plexus, which Geronimo was only partially able to block.

"*Hai!*" The Indian dropped the thug with a hard palm blow to the forehead, and stood panting. Suddenly his legs were jerked from under him by one of the men he had felled earlier.

His three assailants combined forces and he was buried under a tangle of punching and kicking fists and feet. Geronimo was overwhelmed. When he finally admitted it and relaxed, he saw that his captors were men of medium height, swarthy, and black-haired. No doubt Marakis. The tallest one was their spokesman.

"You and the other American—how are you connected with El Sidi's murder?"

Geronimo glared.

"I advise you to talk. Remaining silent will bring on most unpleasant results."

The TEEN agent knew the men were serious. If they were willing to go so far as to torture him, then something must be making them quite desperate. He wanted to know what that something was.

"No connection. My roommate was almost killed instead of him, that's all."

"What do you know of the murderer?"

"Nothing. My friend was the one who stood closest."

The three men held a whispered conference, then their spokesman said, "We want to speak to him. Meet us here at ten tonight and do not try anything foolish. The consequences would be severe."

"I understand."

The men released Geronimo and disappeared into the woods. The Apache turned the Porsche around and drove back to the castle.

On the way, he rubbed his bruised arms with a cunning grin. The Marakis were playing right into their hands! If Valorsky had zapped El Sidi, what was the big beef? Perhaps it had to do with the dead count's records. Maybe tonight's developments would tell.

He could not find Chris anywhere. None of the guests or servants had seen the blond youth in the last hour. Geronimo was perplexed, feeling twinges of concern. He quickly checked the rooms on the ground floor. Then he went up to the second floor to search.

Part way down the hall, the TEEN agent heard loud voices from Lothar's study. He padded silently to the door and listened. He couldn't make out the words, but one of the three voices belonged to Chris. He tried the door gently. It was locked.

The Apache's first thought was to pick it. No.

He had better not. The slightest sound would give him away.

Instead, Geronimo left the hall, went downstairs, and out of the castle. He circled around until he came to a vine-covered trellis which extended up to a point just beneath the balcony off Lothar's study.

Geronimo looked about. A gardener riding a mowing machine clattered by. The Indian ducked out of sight. He'd have to make it up the trellis before the mower returned for the next strip. Now sure that nobody was looking, Geronimo slipped off his loafers and started to climb up the trellis. He raised his hand slowly over the balcony railing and looked through the French doors into the study.

Lothar was waving his fist and speaking angrily to Chris. Beside the count stood Drucker, jabbing his pruning shears toward the TEEN agent!

3 · Moon Wolf

GERONIMO EDGED HIMSELF up over the railing and stole catlike to the partially open doors.

"This is fine repayment for my hospitality," the count was saying. "You have been seen searching rooms where you have no business. I find you in the tower. You harass my servants with questions. What is all this—this *snooping* about?"

Chris attempted a smile. "Herr Graf, I think a misunderstanding has arisen. I haven't been snooping. It's merely that my friend and I find the Schloss fascinating. Perhaps our enthusiasm has caused us to violate good taste. If so, you have our most sincere apologies."

Drucker spoke to Lothar in German, then the

count turned to Chris again. "What were you doing in the park? What did you expect to find?"

"We were interested in the topiary work."

"The topiary indeed!" Lothar reddened, yanked open a desk drawer, and reached inside.

Geronimo couldn't risk the count's pulling a gun. He banged in through the doors, reached the count in two bounds, and pinned his arms behind his back. Drucker rushed forward with the shears. Chris chopped the gardener's wrist and the shears dropped soundlessly on the thick carpet.

The situation was at worst explosive, at best embarrassing. Chris jumped into the breach. "All right," he said. "This has gone far enough. I feel awfully silly, but I'm going to make a clean breast of it. Gerry, I think you can release the count."

Lothar was fuming when Geronimo stepped back.

"Well?"

Chris told him that he was a great detective story fan. He described the light he and Geronimo had seen in the tower, but was careful not to mention anything of the topiary figure of the Ace of Shadows.

"Coming right on the heels of El Sidi's murder," he said, "we thought there might be a connection. I guess we got what we deserved for playing amateur detective."

Lothar was not convinced. "If you are exchange students as you say you are, then you would not mind my checking with the university at Munich?"

Chris shrugged. "Go right ahead."

Lothar made a long-distance call and was connected with the university's department of student records. The conversation was in German. Chris, appearing not to understand, managed to signal Geronimo that their cover was holding up perfectly.

Lothar hung up, looking obviously relieved. "It is true. I am sorry for doubting you. You must forgive my suspicion. You see, something of great value has been stolen from me."

"Stolen?" Chris asked innocently. "What? Perhaps we can help you get it back."

"*Nein, nein.* This is a personal matter." The count rose, guided Geronimo and Chris to the door, and showed them out. "Thank you for your offer. Good-by for now. Accept my apologies for this incident."

The TEEN agents went to their room. Geronimo told Chris of his brush with the Marakis and of their scheduled meeting.

"Think there's much risk?" Chris asked.

"Not now. They want something from us. After they've got it, though, I wouldn't trust them."

Chris nodded. "This 'something of great value'

that's been stolen from Lothar. You think it's the papers?"

"Might be. He's as touchy as a pony with a burr under the blanket."

"A Communist burr? A Maraki burr? TOAD?"

"Your guess is as good as mine."

They arrived at the meeting place precisely at ten o'clock that night. Chris turned out the Porsche's lights and switched off the ignition. A few moments of silence passed, broken only by the hoot of an owl and the croaking of tree frogs. Then the brush crackled a few feet off the road.

"Man," said Geronimo, "they may be great on the desert, but they'd never make the grade at the old reservation! Let's go, *choonday*."

The boys got out of the car and walked a few feet in from the road. A full moon shone low in the sky and the night was brightly illuminated.

The snapping of branches grew louder. Then the three Marakis stepped into view.

"So," said the tallest one, "you have come. It was a wise decision. Your health is insured."

"Great," said Chris. "But what's this all about? I mean, why did you go and stomp all over my buddy?"

The Maraki rubbed his bruised jaw gingerly. "We were not the only ones who stomped. Your friend fights like a lion. We only wished to speak to him."

"You have a strange way of starting conversations," Geronimo growled.

"That is unimportant. Now that you are both here, we ask you again: What do you know of El Sidi's murder?"

"El Sidi's murder," Chris repeated. "Hm! Let me see. Well, it was committed at Count Dietrich von Kronstein's funeral. It was done with a blowgun dart which almost hit me. Guess that's about it."

"Do not toy with us!" the Maraki barked.

Chris matched the Arab's anger. "What do you expect me to do! We're students in a foreign country. We drive to Kronstein to pay our respects to a well-known and loved man who has died—and we get shot at and beat up!"

"There is no need to become upset. Certainly you can understand that we desire to bring our countryman's assassin to justice. We ask your help."

"That's a bit more like it," Chris said. "All right. I'll tell you this. Immediately after El Sidi fell, I saw a young woman rush from the chapel before the doors were sealed."

The Maraki's interest was obvious, but he had reservations, too. "You said nothing to the police about this. Why?"

"We didn't want to get involved."

"Ah, yes. Americans are famous for that." He

leaned forward eagerly. "What did she look like?"

As he and Geronimo had planned, Chris gave them Jessica Valorsky's description. "She was twenty-five years old, or so. Roughly five-foot-four. Pretty. Short black hair, an oval, pixy face. Large dark eyes. Good figure. Long legs. That's all I can tell you."

"Do you realize what he says!" exclaimed one of the Marakis. "It is—"

"Quiet!" snapped the spokesman.

"Was I of some help, gentlemen?" Chris asked.

"Only the future can tell."

"Anything else we can do for you? Go into the village with you and see if I can spot her?"

"No," the Maraki said quickly. "I will report what you have said to our government. They will determine appropriate steps. Thank you. Good night."

Chris and Geronimo returned to their car and started back to the castle. Half a kilometer later, Chris stopped, turned the Porsche around, doused the lights and drove slowly back to the meeting place.

"Now we'll see what they do with that info," he said.

After a few minutes they saw the Marakis' car come out of the underbrush. They followed it into the village. It stopped at a phone booth, dropped one of the Arabs off, and drove away. Chris sat undecided a moment, then he said, "Let's take him."

"*Deeka!*" Geronimo replied in a tight-lipped grin. "Let's go!"

They got out of the Porsche, closed the doors quietly, and walked the half block to the booth. The Maraki's back was to them. He was fishing in his pocket for a coin. The booth door was open.

From his suit pocket Geronimo took a device resembling a ballpoint pen. He leveled it at the Maraki and pressed the clip. *Phhht!* A "sleepy sliver" hit the man in the shoulder and he collapsed. The slim anesthetic dart would keep him out for about an hour.

The TEEN agents sprinted forward. Geronimo shattered the bulb while Chris pulled out the man's passport and wallet. Using a miniature flashlight, they examined the papers. His name was Rezi, obviously a secret agent of the Marak government. They also found a coded list of what appeared to be names. They copied the list, then returned the belongings and propped the man in the booth.

They drove back to the castle and parked the Porsche. But instead of going inside, the boys decided to walk through the park where they could talk without fear of bugging. Wandering past the field, they came to the bank of Lake Kronstein.

Offshore, in the silent shadows of the pine trees, fish were rising to the surface, feeding on night insects.

"We'll mail that list to Sepp first thing in the morning," Chris said. "After that we'll— What's wrong, Gerry?"

The Apache was peering into the shadows. "I don't know. Funny feeling. We're being stalked."

Chris had learned some time ago to trust his friend's Indian instincts. They were rarely wrong. The TEEN agents peered carefully around but saw nothing.

"Maybe my imagination," Geronimo said doubtfully, and they resumed their walk along the edge of the water.

"Behind us!" Geronimo spun suddenly.

Streaking down on them was a huge wolf-like animal. Its fur shone ghostly silver in the moonlight. Its jaws were open, studded with long sharp teeth.

The beast let loose a chilling howl, as its muscles hunched for a spring.

Both TEEN agents were reaching for their anesthetic pens, but Chris realized they would never make it in time. "The lake!" he yelled.

He and Geronimo plunged into the cold water, their breath locked in their lungs. They swam furiously, kicking into the black depths.

4 · An Official Request

CHRIS COOL'S NEED for air was desperate. Clutching the anesthetic pen in his hand, he pumped his way to the surface and gasped in the dank night air.

An instant later Geronimo appeared beside him. They looked around and listened. The beast had gone.

"Whew!" Geronimo said, treading water. "I tangled with some pretty mean lobos on the reservation, but I never saw anything like that before."

"Hungry-looking, wasn't he?"

"Ravenous. Could've polished off two TEEN-burgers in a couple of easy gulps."

"You think he's a Schloss watchdog?"

"We'd have seen him before."

They swam to the bank and clambered out of the water. Their feet squeaked in their wet shoes and their soaking clothes shed drops across the close-cut lawn as they walked to the Schloss.

Lothar was playing chess in a small room off the entrance hall. He saw the boys enter and abandoned his game. Quickly he came to their side. "Are you all right? What happened?"

"We were attacked by an animal," Chris said. "Some sort of dog, or wolf. We had to dive into the lake to escape." He described the beast and how it had apparently been hunting them.

"Wouldn't be a pet of yours, would it?" Geronimo asked.

"I keep no such dangerous creature on the grounds," Lothar said indignantly. "Nor do I know of any in the surrounding country. You are sure you are not exaggerating?"

"We don't go around jumping into lakes for fun!" Geronimo growled. His obsidian eyes were glittering.

Chris knew the Apache's temper was rising. He touched his arm and said, "It's been a long day. I think some sleep will put things back in perspective. Come on, Gerry."

Next day they drove into the village, went directly to the small post office, and sent Sepp a copy of the list they had found in the Maraki agent's pocket.

They wandered through the village, taking advantage of their first true opportunity to sight-see. The streets were narrow and crooked and paved with rough cobblestone. Set close to the curbs, the buildings were of dark wood and tan stucco, peak-roofed. Only few were more than two stories high.

The village men wore rough work clothes. Many of the women, dressed in bright skirts, had their hair in braids.

At the market place they chatted in small groups, casting their eyes about fearfully. Chris and Geronimo pressed close to where three of them were examining fresh-killed rabbits, hung by the hindquarters in front of a butcher's stall.

The boys heard only part of the whispered conversation, but the gist of it was clear. The ghost of Count Dietrich and ravening werewolves were rampant in Kronstein!

In midafternoon the TEEN agents stopped at a table under the large shade trees of an open-air nook behind an inn. After ordering two tall glasses of *Apfelsaft*, they discussed the conversation they had overheard.

"Well, how're you fixed for silver bullets, *kemosabe?*"

"Would you believe poison darts?"

Geronimo made a choking gesture, then became serious again. "Count Dietrich's ghost is walking the town at night. Well, we can write that off to local superstition."

"What about the animal? We saw it, too."

"Maybe it was a hallucination."

"Sure."

They finished the apple cider and went back to the castle.

"Mr. Cool," the butler said, "there is a man waiting to see you. In the drawing room."

An Arab in a tailored suit was seated in an easy chair. He leaped to his feet when the TEEN agents entered. "Mr. Christopher Cool? Mr. Geronimo Johnson?"

"Yes," Chris answered. "What can we do for you?"

"Please." The man took an envelope from his inside jacket pocket and handed it to Chris.

The envelope bore the wax seal of the Marak government. Typed on the heavy bond paper within was a formal invitation from Marak's highest official, Premier Abu ben Dellah, to visit the capital city of Phrates and to recount personally what they had seen at the funeral murder. The waiting Maraki would convey their verbal reply to the consulate.

"The wind shifts," Geronimo said in Apache.

"And I think we should follow the direction," Chris replied.

The Arab frowned at the strange language.

Chris switched to English, thanked the man, and informed him that they would be pleased to accept, but that they could not leave for another day or so. The Maraki salaamed and left.

"Something cooking," Chris said.

"Our goose, maybe," Geronimo answered. "They think we know more."

"Or perhaps too much. I feel we're on the scent of something big, Gerry!"

"Like *Petit Mensonge.*"

"Not as pleasant, but just as exotic. I hear the capital of Marak is the 'in' place for thrill seekers."

The boys went to their room to consult Sepp on this new development and to formulate plans. Chris was just setting the stem of his watch radio to Transmit when a knock sounded on the door.

Geronimo opened it to a tall, large-boned servant with blond hair and a tanned complexion.

"*God kväll,*" the man said in Swedish. "Good evening. I am Gunnar. Count von Kronstein requests seeing you in his study if you are not busy."

The boys left their room and accompanied the servant down to Lothar's study.

"Sit down, please," Lothar said. "It was good of you to come. How are you enjoying Kronstein?"

"Acting like tourists," Chris replied. "Your town is quite ancient. Especially the old market place."

"Ah, then you must have heard the women gossiping."

Geronimo stifled a grin and said, "They seemed scared about something."

"And I can tell you what it is," the count said as Gunnar stood by stiffly. "They are talking about ghosts and werewolves. You see, you were not the only ones to see that terrible beast."

"Might have been only a friendly puppy." Chris tried to laugh it off, but Lothar shook his head seriously.

"*Nein*," he said. "This beast is upsetting our village. Several of my servants have resigned. I am forced to hire new people."

After the TEEN agents had expressed their sympathy, Chris told Lothar that they would be leaving shortly for an overseas trip.

"We want to see as much as we can while we're young," he explained. "Back home—business—marriage—you know all about that, Count."

Lothar managed a grim smile, saying he hoped they would stay long enough to attend a reception the following night. "That is really why I sent for you," he continued. "A visiting author from Berlin, Gerhart Nord, will be with us."

"A fiction writer?" Chris asked. Receiving a nod, he added, "This is a good place for a ghost story!"

"Then you'll attend? It will be quite amusing."

"By all means," Chris said, and Geronimo grunted his assent.

The boys returned to their room. "Pretty callous," said Chris, "having a reception so soon after his father's death." The TEEN agents contacted Sepp and briefed him on what had transpired. Then he asked them to meet him at a spring in a secluded glade midway between the Schloss and the village late the next night. He wanted to show them a photograph of Jessica Valorsky.

The boys went downstairs for dinner and passed the remainder of the evening in idle conversation with other guests. When the hour grew late, they went back to their room, turned off the lights, and waited in darkness for the castle's inhabitants to settle into sleep. They wanted to examine the tower room before leaving for Marak.

The tower might hold a clue to the secret cache of the dead count's records and perhaps the missing Jessica.

"It's been quiet more than an hour," Chris said finally. "Let's go."

Both of them wore black pullover sweaters, black slacks and socks and dark sneakers. They had darkened their skin with carbon. Stealthily they made their way out of the castle and across the grounds to the base of the tower.

"I'll go up," Chris said. "You stand guard here.

If there's trouble, we'll communicate by watch radio."

Geronimo nodded. He helped Chris swing back the large door. "Hey," he said. "Here's something we didn't notice before."

"What?"

"The locks. There are three of them, and each one has been broken."

"Recently, too. There's not a speck of rust on them."

"What do you make of it?"

"Don't know. Maybe the answer's upstairs."

It was dark in the stairwell. Chris trailed his hand along the stone wall as he ascended. It was a long way up and he felt the strain in his legs by the time he reached the landing outside of the tower room.

The door was ajar. Moonlight was streaming into the room, some of it spilling out onto the landing. Chris noted two massive locks on the door. Both of them had been broken.

"Someone's been in here before me," Chris thought. "Maybe looking for something. Like what? The count's records?"

The TEEN agent swallowed hard. An assassin might be lying in wait right now. Was he being suckered into a disaster? Chris pulled back his sleeve to leave his watch unimpeded. He checked his sleepy-sliver pen, took a deep breath, and slipped inside the room.

It appeared to be empty. Chris could not see much and he dug in his pocket for the miniature flashlight.

Then he heard a scuffle behind him. Spinning, the youth caught sight of a dark silhouette. He lunged forward, at the same time reaching for his pen.

Too late he heard a sharp whooshing sound, then felt his nostrils, throat, and lungs burning. Lightheaded, he staggered backward, and knew he was falling.

Chris fumbled with the watch radio. His rapidly failing senses held up long enough for him to move the stem. The continuous distress signal transmission was on.

Then he passed out.

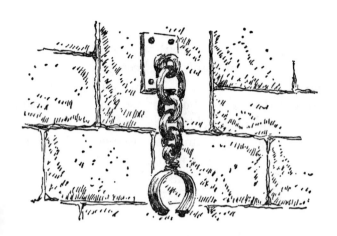

5 · Pulling the Fangs

"BEEP . . . BEEP-BEEP . . ."

Distress signal! Geronimo bolted through the tower doorway and up the stairs. His lips were pulled back in a snarl. If anything had happened to Chris, there wouldn't be enough left of the attacker for the police to identify! There was only one way in and out of the tower. Whoever had jumped Chris was trapped!

When Geronimo reached the landing, he paused, then sprang into the room. He landed in a crouch, poised to strike.

Nobody was there but Chris, motionless on the cold stone floor. Geronimo dropped to his side and pressed his ear to Chris's chest, feeling for a pulse at the same time. Relief flooded over the Apache. Chris's heart was beating strongly.

His buddy probably had been given a whiff of gas, Geronimo thought. By whom? He jumped up and dashed to the window that stood open.

One end of a nylon rope was tied to a metal hook projecting from the casement. Geronimo leaned over to see a man sliding down.

The TEEN agent eased himself through the window, locked his feet around the rope, and slid down.

The man reached the ground seconds before his pursuer and ran toward the topiary garden. Geronimo jumped the last few feet and sprinted after the figure escaping into the shadows of the park.

He moved ahead slowly, suspicious of ambush, at the same time holding his anesthetic pen at the ready. A rustle came from the bushes. Geronimo turned and began advancing cautiously.

Suddenly a chilling growl rumbled in the night. The Apache stopped. Out of the shadows and into the moonlight bounded the savage "werewolf" of Kronstein! The beast bared its fangs and leaped toward Geronimo's throat.

The Indian side-stepped agilely. The animal snapped at empty air, and Geronimo brought it down with a sleepy sliver.

He examined the stunned form briefly, then stood up and looked about.

There was little chance he could find Chris's

assailant now, so he dragged the beast to the base of the tower, fashioned a sling around it with the rope, then climbed hand over hand to the tower.

Chris was just coming to when Geronimo bent over him. "Oh, what a head!" he groaned.

"Did you get a look at the guy?"

"Uh-uh. Only his shadow."

"The Ace of Shadows?"

"Maybe. Don't know."

"Well, it's not a total loss. I nailed the Kronstein werewolf."

"What is it?"

"Some kind of large dog, a little like an Irish Wolfhound. I've never seen the breed before. He'll be out for several hours. I tied him to the end of the rope your playmate escaped on."

Chris read his buddy's mind and grinned. "A little surprise for the castle's occupants."

"Right. Let's haul him up."

They went to the window, double-teamed the rope, and hoisted the beast up over the sill.

"Ugly fellow," Chris remarked. "Hey, Gerry! He's wearing a collar." Chris examined the perforated rolled leather strap, then slit it open with his penknife.

Geronimo wrinkled his nose and sniffed. "*Choonday*, I'm getting a trace of *Petit Mensonge*. Jessica Valorsky's perfume!"

Chris dug further into the collar and came up

with a small piece of perfumed fabric. "Here's the source. Fido must be a special bloodhound on the trail of our girl."

"But what would the Reds want with a TOAD agent?"

"A good question. Maybe we'll find some answers in Marak. But for now let's do what we came to do—have a look around."

The boys flicked on their miniature flashlights and played the pencil-thin beams across the floor and over the walls. Geronimo whistled. "Man, what a setup! It's like an *Ivanhoe* movie."

A variety of chains, manacles, and leg irons were spiked securely to the wall. A few of the locking mechanisms were shiny, as if they had been used recently.

"Someone had a not-too-pleasant stay here," Chris said. "No wonder Lothar didn't want us snooping."

The TEEN agents found nothing more so they called it a night.

Dawn had just broken when the castle's occupants were jarred from sleep by the frantic, echoing barks of the trapped dog. Chris and Geronimo rolled over on their beds, listened to the shouts of consternation and confusion from awakened guests and servants, then grinned at each other and went happily back to sleep.

When they wandered down to breakfast later, they found most of the guests looking bleary-eyed and offering wild theories as to how a dog came to be locked in the tower.

Speculation petered out as the guests prepared for the reception that night. It was a gala affair. An eight-piece string orchestra played continuous waltzes in the Great Hall. Champagne flowed freely as the guests met Gerhart Nord, a short, solid man who kept his listeners laughing over anecdotes from his world travels. "The mystery is the thing," he kept saying. "Always a mystery."

Liveried servants passed among the guests with hors d'oeuvres and canapés on silver trays. As near as Geronimo and Chris could estimate, the guests, speaking various tongues and wearing disparate dress, represented some thirteen distinct nationalities.

The boys split up and worked their way methodically through the groups of guests. There were spies among them, no doubt. Vultures in the world of espionage. They had alighted on the parapets of Kronstein to pluck out Dietrich von Kronstein's dossiers. What a prize for a bird of prey!

Geronimo kept his eyes peeled for any unusual actions, any questionable mannerisms. Chris, under the guise of looking for someone, paused long enough to listen in on Lothar, talking to an elderly man.

"Yes, dear Haller, it is very unfortunate. This will be the last big reception for a while. We can no longer bear the expenses. The family coffers are near empty."

Chris moved on. He met Geronimo at the door to the library.

"Anything?" Gerry asked.

"A blank, except that Lothar says he's broke."

They strolled into the library and idly glanced at the spines of some of the several thousand volumes.

"Quite a collection," Geronimo said. "Philosophy, psychology, comparative religion, art, architecture, history . . . Dietrich von Kronstein must have been an exceptional man."

"Here's something interesting," Chris said. "There's a rather thorough collection on gypsies."

"A special interest."

"Old Dietrich must have liked the roving mystics." Chris examined a few well-worn volumes and put them back. "All authoritative works. None of the popularized junk that most people accept as truth about gypsies. He knew his subject."

The boys spent a little more time browsing, then Geronimo said, "Getting close to the time we're supposed to meet Sepp, *choonday*."

"Let's stall a few minutes. There's a group getting ready to leave. If we slip out with them, our own departure won't be so conspicuous—if anyone's interested."

A small group of guests had congregated

around the twin cathedral-like doors leading out of the castle. Geronimo and Chris blended into it and let themselves be carried out with the general movement. A few paces into the driveway, they split to the side, got into the Porsche, and waited for the last of the cars to pull away.

Chris started the engine and a moment later they were on their way.

The black car sped along, its headlights shafting white cones into the night. Chris handled the wheel expertly. The powerful engine hummed with a steady, pleasing rhythm.

They were rounding a curve when Geronimo yelled, "Look out!"

Chris whipped the wheel to the right, shifted into a lower gear for more power, and jammed the accelerator down.

The driver of the white Volvo evidently panicked. Instead of cutting to his right, he hit his brakes. The car slewed sideways and blocked the road.

Crash!

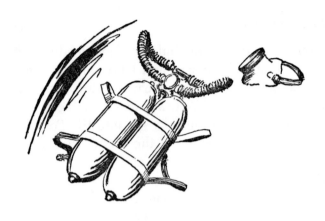

6 · Search and Annoy

THE VOLVO WENT up on two wheels, then over-
turned. Chris and Geronimo were snapped forward against their seat belts. For a dizzying
moment it seemed as if the earth had risen up
in a great convulsion, then came crashing down.

The moment ended. Everything was quiet.

"Gerry, you all right?"

The Apache gingerly probed a lump on his
forehead. "Nothing fatal."

The TEEN agents climbed out of the Porsche
and went to the car they had struck. "Someone's
lying at the edge of the road," Chris said. "Take
a look. I'll check the car."

"Hey, *choonday!*" Geronimo called. "This bird's
wearing a wet suit."

Chris looked into the car and saw another

man, unconscious. He, too, was encased from neck to feet in a skin-tight black rubber suit. The man's eyelids fluttered open and he groaned. Chris helped him to the road beside his companion, who was now sitting up.

Chris spoke in Apache. "There are scuba lungs, face masks, and flippers in the back seat of the car. We might be on to something."

"*Gonzone!* You're right."

The pair were recovering their senses. The heavier one of the two looked up angrily. "You stupid kid," he said in German. "You could have killed us! Whoever taught you to drive should be shot!"

"You'll have to excuse me," Chris said acidly. "I'm not used to ducking cars in the middle of the road. Especially on curves."

The men glared.

"How's the skin diving around here?" Geronimo asked. "Kind of an odd hour for it, no?"

The divers stood up. "What's it to you?" said the heavy one.

"Just curious."

Silently the pair walked to the Volvo, checked on their gear, and seemed satisfied. Then they set about trying to right the car. The TEEN agents lent their shoulders to the effort.

"I'd sure like to know some more about this night diving," Chris said. "It sounds like great sport."

"Heave!" called the slight man.

The Volvo tipped back onto all four wheels and the divers got in. The starter mechanism made a grinding sound for several moments, then the motor coughed to life.

"You don't get the point," Chris said. "Where are you going? We'd like to get in on this operation, or maybe you'd rather talk to the police."

The driver sneered. "There is no law against wearing wet suits, and as far as the accident goes, it is your word against ours. The police can not hold us and you know it." He shifted gears and punched the accelerator savagely. The Volvo's tires squealed on the pavement and the car shot forward.

"Let's follow them," Chris said.

The TEEN agents ran to their battered Porsche. Chris reached for the driver's door, then stopped short. The left front tire had been punctured in the collision and was flat.

"Well, that's the end of that idea," Chris muttered. "Call Sepp and tell him to sit tight."

He got the tools and spare out and jacked up the Porsche's front end while Geronimo radioed their contact. When the Apache had signed off, they changed the tire, pulled out the crumpled fender, and were on their way.

Fifteen minutes later the Porsche turned off the road at a lightning-blasted oak, went several yards into the underbrush, and stopped. Chris and Geronimo got out and walked deeper into the glade.

Sepp was waiting at the side of the spring. He was a ruddy-faced, portly man with bulldog jowls, twinkling eyes, and an air of irresponsible jollity. The least-likely-looking spy imaginable, Chris thought, which made him even more efficient at his trade.

"*Guten Abend, meine Freunde,*" he said.

"*Guten Abend,*" Chris replied. "*Wie geht es Ihnen?*"

"*Danke gut, und Ihnen?*"

"The car's banged up." Chris switched to English. "But we're in good shape."

"I am glad. There may be greater danger ahead. Q has your request on Marak. You must wait for his approval."

"What do you think about it?" Chris asked.

Sepp rolled his eyes. "More is in progress than the search for the records. The Marakis have no use for such documents."

"Some kind of an oil-well deal?" Chris asked.

"Possible. War threats in the Arab lands are more thick—how do you say it?—than the flies. Both Russia and your country agree, for once, that the balance of power should not be upset."

In the distance came the faint drone of a helicopter.

"Maybe the Reds are trying to work an inside deal," Geronimo suggested, looking absent-mind-

edly at Jessica Valorsky's photograph which Sepp
had handed him. The TEEN agent wondered
where the girl might be and which disguise
she was using now.

Sepp nodded. "An inside job? That would not
be a surprise. As soon as Q approves, the CIA
will arrange a contact for you in Phrates."

The noise of the helicopter grew louder. Chris
looked up into the dark sky and frowned. Sepp
and Geronimo followed his gaze. The chopper's
winking running lights approached rapidly.

"Sepp," said Chris, "is there any reason for a
whirlybird to be in this area?"

Sepp stroked his jaw. "*Nein*. It is—"

Suddenly the glade was starkly illuminated by
the brilliant white light of a magnesium para-
chute flare.

"Take cover!" Chris yelled. The three agents
raced for the woods, flung themselves to the
ground, and crawled to tree trunks and fallen
logs for cover.

The helicopter swung in small lazy circles as
if searching for something.

"They've got us pinned but good," Geronimo
rasped.

"Sit tight," Chris commanded.

Minutes later the helicopter broke its search
pattern and sped off to the east. Chris, Geronimo, and Sepp waited to make sure this was not
a ruse, then crawled out from their concealment.

"Nobody knew we'd be here," Chris reflected.

"Somebody's tailing us," Geronimo said. "The Marakis or TOAD."

"Or the Reds. You pay your money and take your choice."

"As I was saying," Sepp remarked with a deadpan expression. "There is much danger in this."

They parted, Sepp for Munich, the boys for Kronstein Castle. In the morning they had a brief radio message from Sepp. Q had okayed the Marak plan and a package was waiting for them at the cheese-and-sausage shop.

After they had eaten, Chris put in a call to the Maraki Consulate, advising that he and Geronimo had finished their business and were ready to leave.

In turn they were informed that the Maraki Embassy in Munich would book a flight to Phrates and that their visas would be ready for pickup at the embassy any time.

"Now what, *choonday?*"

"*Koya,*" Chris replied. "This way."

"The library?"

"*Gonzone.*"

The TEEN agents entered the empty room and Chris went directly to the gypsy collection. "Gerry, I have a feeling there's a clue hidden here." He pulled out a new book, published in New York. As he opened its pages, a gray-haired, wrinkled woman walked in.

"*Ach, entschuldigen Sie,*" she said, and started to back out.

"Don't go," Chris said.

"I wanted a—a book on herbs," she said, embarrassed. "Count Dietrich let me come in here. He was a gourmet, you know."

The woman introduced herself as Helga, pastry maker and long-time chief of the castle's kitchen. She got the book she wanted, then noticed the volume in Chris's hands.

"You like gypsies? So did the count."

"Really?"

"He was a little *verrückt* in the head, I think." Helga spun her forefinger near her temple. "One time the gypsy wagons were all over the Schloss grounds. Why, he even let his son Hasso travel with them."

"Hasso?" Chris grew excited. "I didn't know he had another son."

"*Ja.* Hasso, the eldest. He traveled with the gypsies when he was not in school." She shook her head sadly. "Tch, tch. Such a nice boy."

"Where is he now?" Chris asked.

"Dead. Drowned with a gypsy family many years ago when a bridge collapsed somewhere far to the south."

"Oh." Chris did not let his disappointment show. For a moment, he had thought they were on to something. "I'm sorry."

"If you are interested in gypsies, there is one

that lives in the village. He is too old already to travel with his tribe."

"Thank you, Helga. Perhaps we will talk to him. It's for a term paper I'm writing on nomadic peoples."

The boys left. "I think the old fellow might be worth seeing," Chris said. "Let's visit him as soon as we get back from Phrates."

"What was that business about his 'tribe'? I thought all gypsies were the same."

"No," Chris said. "Only in the sense that all Indians are the same. Otherwise, they're members of tribes—just like the Sioux, Iroquois, Apache, and so on."

"Very sensible," Geronimo said. "Now you're talking my language, *choonday*."

A servant had brought their bags down from the room and placed them in the entrance hall.

Lothar appeared, hastened to his young guests, and shook hands. "*Auf Wiedersehen*," he said. "*Gute Reise*. Have a good trip."

"Thank you, sir," Chris replied. "We've enjoyed your hospitality. It has been a most exciting experience."

The count waved off the compliment. "I am certain you have enjoyed better. Too much evil has happened to spoil your stay. Perhaps I can make it up to you later. Will you honor me with another visit?"

"Looking forward to it," Chris said.

"Maybe sooner than he expects," Geronimo murmured in Apache as the trio stepped out of the castle.

Chris and Geronimo started toward their Porsche, which was waiting in the driveway. Instantly the TEEN agents tightened up, hands moving up to defensive karate positions.

"*Ai,*" Geronimo hissed.

"We're in for it, I'm afraid," Chris replied.

What looked to be an entire platoon of uniformed men was marching directly toward them, grim and determined!

7 · "Beware!"

LOTHAR RAISED HIS hand in greeting. *"Guten Morgen, Herr Leutnant."*

"Guten Morgen, Herr Graf."

"I have requested the aid of the police," Lothar explained to Chris and Geronimo, "in finding my father's will. I have been unable to locate it, and the estate cannot be settled."

The TEEN agents relaxed. "We wish you the best of luck," Chris said. "Good-by, and thank you again for your hospitality."

"Good-by."

The boys carried their bags to the Porsche. Leaving the driveway, Geronimo said, "That was a heart stopper, *choonday*. For a minute I thought the opposition had us but good."

"I wasn't exactly happy myself," Chris admitted.

It was a pleasant, bright day and the forty-kilometer trip to Munich went quickly. Shortly before noon they passed the summer castles outside the city walls, drove through one of the remaining fourteenth-century gates, and entered the old town.

The cathedral, center of Munich's religious life, stood in splendor unchanged in five hundred years. Chris slowed briefly to admire the ancient Town Hall in the Marienplatz before pulling over to the curb on Georgenstrasse in Schwabing, Munich's artists' district. He parked in front of a small shop. Its facade was of heavy old wood and on its dusty window were the words: SEPP KALT-HUBER, KÄSE UND WURST.

A brass bell tinkled when the boys entered the dim, cool store, and they deeply inhaled the pungent spicy aroma of sausages and cheese. The wurst hung from the walls and ceiling, loops and coils of them and large, heavy single pieces. There were great wheels and wedges of black, brown, and yellowish cheese. Some were covered with a mold to delight even the most finicky connoisseur.

A robust blond girl smiled at them from behind a polished counter. *"Guten Tag. Was möchten Sie bitte?"*

"Ist Herr Kalthuber da?" Chris asked.

"*Nein.*"

Chris looked **disappointed**. He explained that he and Geronimo **were** Sepp's nephews, Wunny and Tooey Kingston. **He** wondered if Sepp had left a package for them.

"*Ja, ja.*" The girl hastily brushed back a strand of hair from her forehead and disappeared into the back of the shop. She returned with a parcel wrapped in brown paper and marked "Fragile."

Chris said thanks and asked her to relay their best to Uncle Sepp. "We'll have to get in touch with him later."

In their car Chris concealed the package in a special compartment under the front seat.

"Where to now?" Geronimo asked. "The Marak Embassy?"

"Might as well."

They left the car parked, walked east on Georgenstrasse to Kurfürsten, and turned left. A block later they came to Franz-Joseph Strasse and headed east again.

The Marak Embassy was located a few doors from the corner. It was an inconspicuous building that might never have been recognized as an embassy except for the Marak flag jutting from a second-story window.

Geronimo rang the bell and a butler opened the door. The bulge in his jacket caused the TEEN agents to exchange glances. Why should an embassy butler carry a gun in a shoulder holster?

They were shown into the office of a short, smiling man who greeted them with the enthusiasm and sincerity of a con artist. He gave them their visas, saying they had been booked on a nonstop flight from Munich to Phrates which would depart at noon the next day.

"Upon arrival, you will of course be met by a limousine. The premier is most anxious to speak with you." The official insisted the boys feel free to call if any questions occurred before their departure. Then he wished them a good trip.

In the street, Geronimo said, "Whew. Talk about nests of rattlesnakes! I was as comfortable in there as I would be at my own execution."

Chris nodded. "Whoever the embassy tailor is, he doesn't know much about the art of concealment. I figure roughly half the staff was armed."

"Strange for a so-called friendly nation. *Choonday*, methinks this trip is not going to be much of a holiday."

"A very astute observation, faithful Indian."

Geronimo called Sepp from a phone booth, but their contact was still not in. The boys stopped at a café, drank a demitasse of thick, strong, black coffee, and decided to go for a leisurely stroll in the famed Englische Garten.

They walked to Leopoldstrasse, then down

past the imposing Akademie and the somber Universität to Veterina Strasse and the entrance to the garden.

It was lush—a huge, green, and idyllic oasis in the center of a modern, bustling city. The landscaping was enchanting, the clear brooks and streams a refreshing sight. The TEEN agents relaxed on a bench.

"What is so rare as a day in Bavaria?" Chris said, stretching his arms behind his head. "Hey, look over here!"

A barefoot old woman hastened toward the boys. She wore dangling earrings and a deep-colored, ankle-length dress hung with gold ornaments. Her dark hair was set in long braids, which softened the lines of her wrinkled face.

"The old one knows you, *choonday*."

"Not me. She's looking at you."

Chris saw anxiety in the woman's eyes as she stopped before them and said, "*Droboy tume Romale*."

It was a traditional gypsy greeting. Chris, who had studied gypsies and their language, gave the appropriate answer. "*Nais tuke*."

"I will read your future," she said quickly and seized Chris's left hand. Her large eyes widened. "The journey you have planned might mean death!"

Chris frowned. The old woman dropped his hand. She took Geronimo's. "Beware!" she rasped, and pressed a soft piece of material into the Apache's hand. She closed his strong, slender fingers over her gift, then darted off before the boys could question her.

Geronimo shook his head. "What do you think? Was she trying to frighten us or warn us?" He opened his hand to examine the piece of colorful cloth with a knot tied in the middle.

"That's a Dead Man's String!" Chris exclaimed.

"A what?"

"Gypsies," Chris explained, "or the Rom as they call themselves, take the measurements for a man's coffin with a narrow length of flowery cloth. After the funeral they cut it into short lengths and tie a knot in the middle of each piece."

"Some kind of magic?"

Chris nodded. "To be used only against the Gaje, or non-gypsies, who have always persecuted the Rom."

"Like how?"

"If in danger, the gypsy unties the Dead Man's String, calls the name of the deceased and says, 'Sweet dead one, let the noose about to be tied around my neck be undone.'"

"I respect their customs," Geronimo said gravely. "*Choonday,* this is a serious warning."

"I think you're right. Could she be a friend of the old count?"

The Apache shrugged as they left the Englische

Garten and started across the Luitpold Bruecke to the opposite bank of the Isar River.

They had walked half the length of the bridge when shouts and the sound of a horn caused them to turn.

"*Ai,*" Geronimo said softly. The old gypsy was lying crumpled and bloodied in the street. The TEEN agents went racing back.

Two policemen were beside the woman, one kneeling. He looked up and told his partner that she was dead. A bystander pushed forward and spoke excitedly to the officers. The gypsy had been killed, he said, by a car with a Corps Diplomatique license plate. He remembered the number. Chris wrote it down.

The boys drifted away from the crowd. Geronimo fingered the Dead Man's String. "She was murdered. I'll stake my arm on it."

"For warning us?"

"Looks that way. We must be cautious."

It was growing late, but neither boy had an appetite. They got their car, checked in at their hotel, and phoned Sepp. He was back.

In a coded conversation he told them to evade the government delegation at the Phrates airport. They were to go directly to their CIA contact. Sepp explained where they would find him and how he could be recognized. Before signing off, he promised to check on the license number of the death car, and advised the boys to study their package carefully.

With the door and balcony window of their room secured, Chris unwrapped the package. The contents had been put together by Pomeroy, the fussy little genius of TEEN's technical staff—affectionately referred to as the "Department of Dirty Tricks."

Chris drew out a coded sheet of instructions. It began: *This will disintegrate in five minutes, so read carefully and rapidly.*

"Very nice," Chris said when they had finished.

Pomeroy had already fashioned a considerable arsenal for the TEEN agents. It included anesthetic pens, snooperscopes, smoke and equipment-rusting grenades, rocket-hopper shoes and wrist-watch radios.

"Ah, look at this new stuff," Chris said.

"Beautiful."

Their equipment had been supplemented with four cuff buttons, which in reality were nostril gas masks, two small vials of a potent knockout gas to be concealed in special shirt-cuff pockets; two plastic explosives and twin ruby rings with miniature electronic devices to detonate the explosives.

The powerful little bombs were one-inch strips with adhesive backs. They were to be hidden behind the agents' ears. Pomeroy had been careful to match the skin colors of each boy.

"Never can tell when we'll need another dirty trick," Chris said as the young spies adjusted their new weapons.

"Careful with that ring," Geronimo replied. "A wrong twist and your head will go into orbit."

Chris nodded. He locked the ring in safety position just as the instruction sheet smoked and turned to ashes.

The boys ordered a light meal from room service and reviewed their instructions while they ate. A porter cleared the empty tray, and the boys went to bed.

Though their flight didn't leave until twelve, they woke up early as usual. They decided to have breakfast, then contact Sepp and see if he had been able to trace the car.

They were about to leave when a knock sounded on the door. Geronimo opened it. A tall good-looking girl in an attractive summer dress stood there. She looked embarrassed when she saw Geronimo.

"Oh . . . I'm so sorry. I must have the wrong room number."

Chris, who was tightening his tie before the mirror, turned his head when he heard the sound of his native tongue.

At that moment the balcony window crashed in. Two rough-looking thugs landed on the carpet.

8 · Knockout!

CHRIS AND GERONIMO whirled to meet the attack. Amazingly, the intruders just stood there and smiled.

"*Choonday*," Geronimo gasped. "I can't . . ." The Apache sagged unconscious to the floor.

Chris's head was splitting. His arms hung leaden at his side and his legs refused to move. There was an acrid smell in his nostrils. *The girl*, he thought foggily.

He turned his head. She was still standing there, beaming just as pleasantly as before. Only one thing had changed. Now she was holding a gas gun in her hand.

He tried to stagger toward her. She gave him another whiff of the gas.

"Nighty-night," she said.

Then everything went black and Chris felt as if he were falling, falling endlessly through darkness. . . .

Chris was lying on his back when he awoke. He felt cold metal around his wrists. Handcuffs! He tried his legs. They were roped securely together. What was that roaring noise? He noted that the floor did not seem exactly solid beneath him.

Geronimo was beside him, blinking his eyelids in the first stage of regaining consciousness.

Chris's rapidly clearing senses told him they were in an airplane.

He sat up. Leaning against the cabin wall was a baldheaded, clean-shaven man, holding an automatic pistol loosely in his hand. He grinned at Chris. Beside him stood another man, surly looking and also armed.

Geronimo sat up, shaking his head. "What's the drill, *choonday?*"

"We've been snatched," Chris answered. "And we're being taken somewhere."

The sound of their voices brought forth a low, ominous growl. A great shaggy form padded from behind a crate and glared at them.

"Well, well," Geronimo said. "It's our favorite werewolf. How did a nice doggie like you get mixed up with a rough crowd like this?"

The dog growled again, louder.

The bald man said, "You mistreated my little

pet. You wounded his dignity. He will not forget this."

Both boys recognized the voice immediately.
"Drucker!" they said in unison.

The bald man bowed. "The very same. I look
much better without that horrid red wig and
false beard, don't you think?"

"Not to mention those pruning shears," Chris
said.

"Quite so."

"Now that we're all safely kidnapped and
covered with guns," Geronimo remarked, "how
about taking these cuffs and ropes off? My cir-
culation at the moment is nonexistent."

Drucker laughed. "My good American savage,
this is not a game you are playing with some
amateur."

"I know that," Geronimo said. "But my limbs
are about to fall off just the same."

"At least remove the leg ropes," Chris said.
"At this altitude it's not likely that we'll run very
far."

"Very well. I suppose a certain respect as
professionals is due even to one's enemies. But do
not try anything foolish."

"We won't," Chris said. "But what makes you
think we're your enemies?"

Keeping his gun leveled at them, Drucker took
a penknife from his pocket and cut loose the ropes
around their ankles. "Because you are agents

either of TOAD or the Marakis. That, by definition, makes you my enemies."

"Who are you?" Geronimo asked.

"Just a simple gardener." Drucker laughed.

"Boy, have you got us wrong," Chris said.

"So? Tell me how. I would be interested to
hear."

Chris shrugged. "There's not much to tell.
What you've done is to kidnap two American
exchange students. Our government is going to
raise an awfully big fuss, and your government—
whichever one it is—is not going to be happy with
you."

"I am disappointed," Drucker said. "I expected
something more inventive."

Chris shook his head. "I guess people like you
always find the truth rather flat and uninterest-
ing."

"All you have to do is check with the university in Munich," Geronimo suggested. "They'll
give you the story."

"We checked with them at the very beginning.
Of course you are enrolled there. But even the
clumsiest intelligence agency could have arranged
that."

Chris feigned exasperation. "Would you believe advance invasion scouts from the planet
Venus?"

"I would not." It was obvious that Drucker was
growing impatient.

The boys had no choice but to stick to their cover. "Come on, Drucker," Geronimo said. "This whole thing is growing absurd. I don't know what your game is—in fact, I don't even want to know—but you should be a bright enough guy to realize you've made a mistake. All we want is to—"

"Shut up!" Drucker roared. "I am weary of this idiocy."

"Good," Chris said calmly. "Are you going to take us back to Munich now?"

"You are on your way across the Iron Curtain. Once we land, it will not be long before you are persuaded to give us the details of the Marak deal."

The Marak deal! A hint of something concrete at last. Chris decided to goad Drucker into revealing more. "You can't get anything out of us on that subject."

"Do not be so sure. Let us start with Jessica Valorsky."

A call from the pilot's cabin interrupted the interrogation momentarily. Drucker walked to the front and Chris spoke rapidly to Geronimo in Apache.

"We've run out of time, buddy. The party's getting rough. Get those new plugs in your nostrils if you can. I'm going to knock these guys out with Uncle Pomeroy's beddy-by gas."

"Oh, great! I haven't got them. Must have lost

them in the scuffle at the hotel. You'll have to go it alone. Here comes our friendly gardener."

Drucker seized Geronimo's long, black hair and pointed a knife at his throat. He yanked the Apache's head back. "Speak in English!"

Chris deftly worked the plugs from his shirt cuffs. He faked a sneeze and inserted the miniature air filters into his nostrils. Then he broke the gas capsule and prayed that the anesthetic worked as fast as Pomeroy claimed.

"Where is Jessica Valorsky?" Drucker screamed.

Geronimo sneered, "What would you give to know?"

Drucker looked as if he were on the verge of slicing Geronimo's throat. Then he began to blink. Confusion crossed his face. A moment later he pitched unconscious to the floor. Geronimo passed out at the same time.

A few feet away the huge, gray dog wobbled three steps, then collapsed. The remaining guard sprang to his feet in alarm. He grew pale and slumped down the cabin wall, the gun falling from his hand.

Chris found the keys to the handcuffs in Drucker's pocket. He freed himself and Geronimo, then frisked Drucker thoroughly. He found a Russian passport with Drucker's photograph. The name beneath the photo was Alexi Katabian.

Suddenly the airplane pitched to the left and began a slow dive. The gas had reached the pilot!

Struggling to keep his balance, Chris made his way forward.

He pushed the pilot from his chair and took the controls. Pulling back on the wheel, he brought the plane out of its dive. After spending a few minutes plotting their position, Chris set a new course and banked the plane, heading back toward Munich.

Knowing that other Red agents would be dispatched to investigate when the plane failed to pass its checkpoints en route over the Iron Curtain, Chris decided to set it down in a field a few miles from Munich. This way they would not have to worry about ambush at the airport or about explaining their unscheduled landing.

He was cruising at an altitude of six hundred feet, looking for a likely spot to touch down, when he heard a curse and a grunt behind him. He turned his head and looked back into the cabin. Geronimo and Drucker had come to at the same time. Drucker lunged for his gun.

The Apache knocked it from the Red's hand with a chop to the wrist, then kayoed him with a blow across the back of his neck.

Geronimo made an OK sign to Chris with his thumb and forefinger. Then he went to the second Red, squeezed a pressure point just as the man was regaining consciousness, and sent him off to dreamland again.

Now the dog began to twitch. Geronimo improvised a muzzle and a hobble from the ropes that had bound the TEEN agents' ankles. He secured the dog, then came forward. "How're we doing, *choonday?*"

"Just about to set down. That hayfield looks good to me. Ready?"

Geronimo braced himself. "Let's go."

Chris nosed the plane down in a long, smooth approach. The wheels skimmed the top of the hay.

"Look out for the arroyo!" Geronimo shouted.

A ditch, overgrown with weeds, not visible from the air, had appeared in front of them. Chris pulled back on the wheel.

The plane rose. A shed stood at the end of the hayfield.

"We're not going to make it," Chris said tensely. "Hang on!"

The windshield was filled with the sight of old, weathered boards.

Crash!

9 · The Wayward Cab

"GERRY, ARE YOU all right?"

"I'm not dead."

Chris's ears were still ringing as he looked about. The right wing had been torn off. The propeller was gone. The windshield was shattered. The plane was lying on its side and the shed was demolished.

A quick examination showed their passengers were still breathing. The boys tied them securely.

Chris looked at his watch. It was nine-fifteen. "Less than three hours to take-off. We'd better hotfoot it, Gerry. There's an *Autobahn* on the other side of those trees."

"*Deeka!*"

They jogged through the woods to the *Autobahn*. Chris tried to flag down a car. Several ignored him, but finally a truck stopped and the driver asked the boys if they were in trouble. Chris told him in German that they were students on a holiday and were going back to Munich. The man was sympathetic. His own son was a student, too. He told the youths to hop in.

When they reached the city, Chris thanked the man profusely. The boys leaped out of the truck, grabbed a taxi, and went directly to their hotel.

Chris called Sepp on his wrist-watch radio.

"Where are you? At the airport?" Sepp asked.

"No. We just came back from a little joy ride and had to pick up our bags. We'll be on our way presently, though."

Chris recounted the events of the morning and asked their contact to call the authorities and have the police pick up Katabian and his cohorts.

"Pretty unfortunate situation you got yourselves into," Sepp said thoughtfully. "I will see what I can do. Call me back from the airport."

"Will do."

"Incidentally," Sepp went on, "we've traced the number of the Corps Diplomatique car that killed the old gypsy woman."

"Maraki?"

"Yes."

"I had a hunch it would be. Well, that's one more score to settle with our Arabic friends."

Chris signed off and they quickly left the hotel, drove to the airport, and reached the terminal with only minutes to spare.

They parked the Porsche and tried to contact Sepp by radio. Too much interference from planes taking off and landing at the busy airport made this impossible. They found a phone booth at the edge of the parking lot and Chris dialed the wurst shop.

"Hello, Uncle Seymour? . . . Wunny here. We made it. Not too late for our vacation after all. Did they pick up the sausages at the farm?"

Sepp's voice had the hollow metallic sound of doom. "A bad deal, *mein* nephew. No wurst. None at all. The farmer listened too much to idle chatter and believed it."

"And the dachshund?"

"*Auch weg.*"

"Too bad. Don't worry. There is more knockwurst. *Auf Wiedersehen.*"

Chris hung up and turned to Geronimo. "Those rats talked the naive farmer into freeing them. The police came up with nothing."

"I take it Fido's gone, too."

"Arf-arf. Well, we haven't seen the last of those Red herrings."

"*Ai!*" The Apache nodded.

A man from the Marak Embassy ran to greet them when they came to the Air Marak ticket counter. He looked as if their arrival had just saved him from an ulcer attack. He rushed them down to the field, where the big jet stood, its engines roaring. Their escort hustled them aboard, then walked off sighing and mopping his forehead.

They flew southeast from Munich over Austria, Yugoslavia, Greece, Turkey, Israel, and Jordan. They followed the border between Iraq and Saudi Arabia a while, then swung over the northern end of the Persian Gulf, up toward the Caspian Sea. The pilot announced first in Maraki, then French, German, and English that touchdown at Phrates was estimated in forty-five minutes.

"Let's go over it once again," Chris said in Apache. "What's the first thing we do at the terminal?"

"Clear our passports fast, then dodge the welcoming committee. And how do we do that, *choonday?*"

"By any means possible. When the heat's off, we . . ."

"Take a taxi to the Hotel Sabar and walk from there to . . ."

"The Marak International Bank," Chris answered. "Which elevator do we take, and where?"

"The last express elevator. To the top floor. Our contact is . . ."

"The elevator operator. How do we recognize him?"

"He has a mole on his left earlobe."

The jet landed on schedule. Chris and Geronimo got a position in the front of the line queuing up before the immigration officers.

"Ah, Mr. Cool and Mr. Johnson," said the man who examined and stamped their passports. "A delegation awaits you in the main terminal."

"Fine," Chris said. "But is there a—uh—a washroom in here where we can freshen up?"

"Around the corner. There."

"Thank you."

The TEEN agents turned the corner. The men's room was halfway down a narrow corridor. At the corridor's end was another door, marked EXIT in Arabic.

"That's the one we want," Chris said.

They walked quickly to the end of the hall. Geronimo eased the door open a crack and peeked out. "Soldier with automatic weapon standing guard," he whispered. He took his anesthetic pen, aimed, and dropped the soldier with a sleepy sliver of an hour's potency.

"Nice work," Chris said. "He won't have the faintest idea what happened."

They slipped through the door, stepping over the unconscious soldier. Furtively they worked their way around the outside of the terminal.

"We'd better move fast," Chris said. "They're going to come looking before long."

They reached the edge of the parking area and were dismayed to see no taxis. "Wait!" Geronimo exclaimed. "There's one in the shade of that overhang. See?"

The driver was leaning against a wall, looking morose. His brown face brightened immeasurably when he saw the boys approaching. "Taxi, *effendis?* Taxi?"

"Yes," Chris said. "Take us to the Hotel Sabar, please."

"Most definitely. Be assured of a pleasant ride, sirs."

The gears shifted with a grinding sound. The engine clunked loudly, only four of its six cylinders functioning. It was hot. The sun glared down on arid fields which men, women, and children were working with hand tools.

Finally the scalloped walls and the spiraling towers of Phrates appeared. The taxi entered the city and was soon deep into a sweltering, incredibly impoverished section.

"Driver," Chris said, "this isn't the way to the Hotel Sabar, is it?"

"No, *effendi.* Is *casbah*, native quarter. Interesting to see."

"That may be," Geronimo said. "But right now we want to go to the hotel."

"Please to differ, *effendi.* You want to be right here."

"It's too hot to argue," Geronimo muttered. "So I'm just going to conk you one and drive the cab myself."

"That would not be wise, *effendi*."

"Why not, hotshot?"

"Please to look behind."

The boys glanced out the rear window. Natives were shrinking back from the street in terror. The source of their fear was a jeep following the taxi—and the 50-caliber machine gun mounted on the jeep.

"I see your point," Chris said. Geronimo sat and glowered.

"That is good." The driver tossed two dirty burnooses into the back seat. "Put these on."

The TEEN agents did so, Geronimo making no secret of his anger. When they were dressed, a casual observer could not distinguish them from native Arabs.

The taxi and the jeep made their way through a series of dark, winding streets. They stopped in front of a dingy building.

"Out," the driver said. "Please to go inside." Covering them with a Mauser machine pistol, he guided them up a rickety flight of stairs and into a small room.

Lying on the floor was a man who was bound and gagged. The driver left, locking the boys into the room with the other prisoner. Geronimo tried the door, but it would not give. He was about to shoulder it open when Chris said, "Wait, Gerry. Let's see what we have here."

They both went to the man on the floor, loosened his bonds, and untied the gag.

The man, a slender swarthy fellow dressed in a uniform, rolled over and sat up. He chafed his wrists and ankles.

"Thank you," he said in accented English. "I was close to choking."

"Who did it?" Geronimo asked.

The man shrugged and rose to his feet.

"Who are you?" said Chris. Suddenly he noticed a mole on the man's left earlobe. He shot a second question. "What's that uniform?"

The Maraki frowned at the rapid-fire interrogation and gestured helplessly.

"My name is Yussef. I am an employee of Marak International Bank Building. This is an elevator operator's uniform."

"Do you run an express car?" Geronimo asked.

"Yes. How do you know?"

"We're Wunny and Tooey Kingston," Chris said. "A friend of yours—our Uncle Seymour—asked us to look you up."

"Is your Uncle Seymour keeping his records any better these days?"

"Unfortunately, no."

Mutually satisfied as to their identities, the trio shook hands. "What happened?" Chris inquired.

Their contact was about to answer when a deep voice from behind a curtain at the far wall said:

"*Na may kharunde kai tshi khal tut.*"

"That's Romany!" Chris exclaimed. "Gypsy!"

His mind translated with the lightning speed of a computer. *Do not scratch where it does not itch.*

He and Geronimo streaked to the curtain and plunged behind it.

10 · Pyramid of Danger

THE TEEN AGENTS crashed into an L-shaped sleeping alcove. But nobody was there. Cautiously the boys searched under the low couches.

"Nothing," Geronimo growled. "What gives here, *choonday?*"

Chris inclined his head toward a balcony. "He must have been outside."

Geronimo muttered something under his breath. The boys returned to the room and found their contact missing! The door had been unlocked and was now hanging open.

"The oldest gimmick in the book," Chris groaned, "and we fell for it!"

"Think it's a trap?"

"Could be."

The boys stayed close to the wall and moved out of the room with care, holding their anesthetic pens at the ready.

The hall was empty. The building itself was quite old, decaying. No one lived there. Chris and Geronimo went through each room, searching for their contact. No luck.

"This is more confusing than a paleface's treaty," Geronimo growled.

"Granted. We might as well get out of here while we still can."

They went down the stairs to the alley and then out into the street. It was swarming with natives and beasts of burden. Shopkeepers were arguing violently with turbaned customers. Maimed and crippled beggars abounded.

"Look!" Geronimo hissed. "This country is rich with oil, but the government won't give a penny to the people."

Chris nodded. Though the blond youth could get along in Arabic, the common people of Marak spoke in a strange dialect. He tried without success to ask directions out of the quarter.

"If we'd only thought to bring a street map," he said, angry with himself.

"Won't need one. Look there!"

A squad of Maraki soldiers was double-timing up the street. They were led by a lieutenant, an impatient and harried man, who carried an American issue .45 automatic in his hand. Natives scrambled out of their way.

The lieutenant shouted something at Chris and Geronimo. When the boys did not respond, he called his men to a halt. The soldiers leveled their guns.

The lieutenant addressed the boys in French, then in English.

"You two! Remove your hoods, quick!"

The TEEN agents complied. Chris's blond hair and light complexion marked him immediately as a foreigner.

"Aha!" the lieutenant said. "English or American?"

"American," Chris answered.

"And your friend?"

"An original American. Indian."

Geronimo raised his hand. "How."

"*How?* How what?" The officer frowned.

"Never mind," Chris said.

The man smiled thinly. "Our interrogators will relate it later. We do not take the appearance of foreign weaponry on our streets lightly."

"You mean the jeep and machine gun?"

"You admit your guilt?"

"On the contrary. It was used to kidnap us."

The lieutenant sneered.

"If we reach for our passports, will you tell your men to rest their fingers lightly on their triggers? They look nervous."

The Maraki spoke to his soldiers.

Chris and Geronimo gave their passports over, and the officer flipped them open. His eyes widened. "In the name of Allah! The entire military and police force have been searching for you two. Come, to the premier with all haste! I will be promoted for this!" He summoned a car.

En route to the Royal Palace, Geronimo spoke in Apache. "The decoy words of the gypsy—what do they mean?"

"'Do not scratch where it does not itch.' An old saying of the Rom."

The TEEN agents speculated on its significance. Chris felt it meant that there was nothing to interest them in Marak, and that they should return to Bavaria where all the action was. But who had spoken the words? And why?

The car stopped and the TEEN agents were ushered into the magnificent colonnaded palace. Their escort showed them through many interior courtyards, where water babbled gently from Moorish fountains. The scent of jasmine was everywhere. The boys were left to wait alone a few minutes before an aide arrived to escort them to the premier.

Abu ben Dellah received the Americans in a rather sparsely furnished room. Its floor was covered by a large Persian rug of intricate design. An inlaid desk sat near one wall. Across from it were four wooden and slung-leather chairs.

The Maraki head of state greeted the boys with polite cordiality, then asked how it was that the airport delegation had missed them.

Chris spoke vaguely of taking a wrong turn, becoming lost, and deciding to taxi to the palace. He recounted the kidnapping, but omitted the role of the gypsy and the presence of their CIA contact.

"It's very confusing," Geronimo added. "I can't understand why anyone would want to kidnap us."

"I am sure our police will determine the answer soon. They are most efficient." There was the hint of a threat in the premier's voice.

"I certainly hope so," Chris said innocently. "It was a frightening experience."

"Tell us, please, what you know of Jessica Valorsky."

"Who?"

"Jessica Valorsky."

Chris wrinkled his brow. "Gerry, do you know anyone with that name?"

Geronimo thought a moment. "I know a Jessica O'Brien. She's a sorority president at Rider."

"Sorry," Chris said to the premier. "We can't help you."

The Maraki studied them speculatively. Finally he said, "No matter. Let us turn to the assassination of El Sidi."

Chris told precisely the same story he had on

the night that he and Geronimo had met with the Maraki agents. When he described the girl he claimed to have seen leaving the chapel, the premier nodded.

"Is that all of it?" Dellah asked.

"Yes, Your Excellency."

"I see. Thank you. Would you mind stepping back into the courtyard a moment while I confer with my aide?"

"Of course." When Chris stood up, he dropped a transistorized microphone—half the size of a dime—onto the floor. It would never be noticed against the pattern of the rug.

The TEEN agents went to the courtyard and sat on the edge of a fountain, pretending to admire the small, iridescent fish that were swimming in the pool in slow, lazy circles.

A thin antenna wire was sewn into Chris's collar in a series of repeating loops. The right collar button was a sensitive receiver. Chris adjusted the volume so that he and Geronimo could hear, but so that it was not loud enough to attract the attention of anyone who might be spying.

Premier Dellah's voice came through clearly. "I think we can no longer escape the conclusion that Jessica Valorsky has betrayed us."

"I agree," said his aide. "The question is whether she was seeking personal gain or executing TOAD orders."

The premier laughed unpleasantly. "TOAD

agents follow orders. The consequences of independent behavior are quite horrible. I have seen several examples."

"But we had an agreement. Why would TOAD alter things now?"

"They want our gold, but they do not want to give us—"

Crr-runk. Someone had stepped on the microphone!

For a few moments the boys received only static.

Then they heard the aide say "—know too much already. Show them our oil wells tomorrow."

"Yes, sir," answered the lieutenant who had found them.

A door opened. Chris quickly tuned out the receiver. The lieutenant appeared and told them the premier would like to say good-by.

They returned to the room, where Premier Dellah thanked them most heartily. He said he had arranged a sight-seeing tour for his visitors the next day.

Stammering slightly, Chris asked Dellah for his autograph.

The premier smiled benignly. "Of course."

Eagerly Chris took a pen and memo book from his pocket. The pen slipped from his hand. He bent over to retrieve it—and neatly scooped up the bug at the same time.

After Dellah signed his name with an egotistic

flourish, the lieutenant drove the boys to their hotel. He said he would call for them at eight the next morning.

Closing the door to their room, Chris said, "Well, that was exciting. I've never met a head of state before."

"Me neither," Geronimo answered. "I think I can use some of this trip in a term paper I'm writing."

They kept up a stream of casual collegiate chatter, while they went over the room for bugs. Geronimo found the first one in the phone. Chris found the second in the scrollwork of the bedpost. The third was in the table lamp. There were, all told, six separate listening devices.

Geronimo said in Apache, "*Choonday*, we're wired better than RCA."

Chris nodded and said, "We'll have to stay on guard tomorrow. But for now, let's not give them reason to be any more suspicious. We'll speak in English and limit our conversation to courses, professors, and parties."

Geronimo switched to English. "You know, we're going to have a lot of work to make up when we get back. Especially in that Western History course . . ."

The lieutenant picked them up the next morning and drove them to a small, noncommercial airport where government planes were hangared. The TEEN agents took note of the tight security guard. For a supposedly "free nation" Marak was shockingly militaristic.

It was a short flight, only a little over seventy miles from Phrates, in a small, four-seater plane. Their guides were the lieutenant and an official of the Marak International Oil Company. They landed at the edge of a vast oil field.

Next to the airstrip was a thirty-foot pyramid of immense black conduits, each weighing several tons.

"Those are used to channel the oil across the desert to refining stations," the lieutenant explained. "They are quite interesting."

Chris and Geronimo walked over to examine them, as their guides seemed to wish them to do. The TEEN agents stared up at the giant pipes, impressed.

Suddenly Chris shouted, "Gerry, look out!"

With a great grinding noise, the pyramid of pipes had shifted, and the uppermost ones were tipping toward the boys!

11 · Down in Flames

THE CONDUITS SEEMED to hang suspended a moment, then they came roaring down. Running was useless. The boys would be crushed before they could reach safety.

"Into the air!" Chris yelled.

The TEEN agents leaped up, clicked their heels together, which activated the propulsion jets in their rocket-hopper shoes, and went soaring skyward.

The landslide of pipes rolled over the spot where they had been standing. The jet-assisted jump carried them over the conduits and several yards behind. They came to the ground not far from the plane.

The lieutenant and the oil official had drawn well away when the youths had moved unsuspectingly into the trap. Now the lieutenant yanked his side arm from its holster.

Chris and Geronimo sprinted to the plane and leaped inside. Chris dropped into the pilot's seat and started the engine.

A bullet pinged on the cowling. The lieutenant was closing in fast, his face livid. A squad of soldiers raced in from a guard shack at the end of the field.

"Come on, *choonday*," Geronimo said, "or our scalps will be hanging from Maraki tepees tonight."

Two rifle slugs ripped through the fuselage.

Chris gave the engine full throttle. The plane rolled down the strip, picking up speed, then lifted smoothly into the air.

At an altitude of two hundred feet, Chris said, "They'll be on the radio in less than a minute. Maraki fighters will be all over the sky."

"Can we make it to Teleman?"

"I don't know. It'll be a close race."

Teleman was Marak's neighbor. The two countries were traditional enemies and the Telemanians would be delighted to grant sanctuary to any fugitive from the Maraki government.

Chris flew the plane down on the deck. It was a risky altitude, but since they wanted to avoid detection by Maraki radar they had no choice.

The blond youth followed the contour of the

land, hugging the level stretches of desert, rising gently over small hills, dipping into ravines and steering expertly between cliffs.

Frequent bursts of Maraki dialect from the radio indicated that squadrons of pursuit planes were airborne.

Geronimo was silent, his face impassive, as it always was in a crisis. His eyes swept a mountain range on the horizon.

"So far so good," Chris said. "If we can make it to the foothills on the other side, we'll be in Telemanian territory. Ten more minutes, that's all we need."

Geronimo nodded.

Five minutes later an excited voice from the radio repeated *Teleman* several times.

"They're on to us," Geronimo muttered.

They had just entered the mountains and it was unlikely the plane could reach the Telemanian border before the Maraki fighters intercepted them.

"There's a ledge at seven o'clock," Geronimo said speculatively. "If you can put her down, how about a dead man's ruse?"

"It's either dead man's ruse, or dead man for real. Looks tight, but let's go."

It was a short, narrow cliffside ledge several hundred feet above a deep and rocky gorge. Chris brought the aircraft lower, leveled off, chopped the power as they approached.

The wheels touched, lifted, touched again and the blond agent laid hard on the brakes. Both boys were tight-mouthed as the plane screeched closer to the ledge of the precipice. They stopped with only a few feet to spare.

"Whew!" said Chris.

"Amen!"

They climbed out, quickly drained a few gallons of the high-octane fuel from the wing tanks, and doused it over the engine cowling. After Geronimo put a match to it, they rolled the plane off the end of the cliff.

It went crashing and disintegrating down the mountainside to the bottom of the ravine. There it lay, a ball of fire, billowing black smoke.

The whine of jets overhead sent Chris and Geronimo ducking for cover. Three Maraki fighters screamed earthward, buzzed the wreckage, climbed, then came back for another pass. Satisfied that the boys could not have survived such a wreck, the Maraki pilots flew off.

Geronimo watched them go. "We did it!"

"By a hair."

"That, in the case at hand, is sufficient."

Checking their direction by the sun, the agents struck out toward Teleman. It was slow, hard going, but by nightfall they had descended to the foothills. Half an hour later they found a Telemanian border outpost, identified themselves to the soldiers on duty, and were driven to a small military installation not far away. From there they were transferred to the capital city by helicopter.

Chris and Geronimo went directly to the American Embassy and were received by the ambassador. The soft-spoken Bostonian was grave. "I'd advise an abundance of caution," he said. "Five years of being a neighbor of the Marakis have taught me that they make exceptionally dangerous enemies."

The ambassador arranged to have the TEEN agents flown from Teleman back to Munich after the boys had had a good night's sleep.

En route from the Munich airport to Sepp's "Salami Palace," as Geronimo called it, the boys discussed the Maraki government's curious silence.

"Doesn't seem like them to miss an opportunity to make propagandistic hay," Chris said. "It's a great chance to toss around all sorts of anti-American slogans."

"We must have touched on a very hush-hush deal," Geronimo commented.

"What does TOAD have that Marak is willing to trade gold for?"

"If you can answer that one," the Apache said, "I'll be more than happy to give you an A-plus for the day."

Sepp was in, and the sight of his smiling face

and roly-poly figure was a pleasure for the boys.

"So," he said, "the travelers have returned. Any souvenirs? Perhaps an oil well?"

"We nearly got a ton of pipe on the noggin," Chris said, and related in detail what had happened.

"Who is this strange gypsy?" Sepp muttered.

"I don't know, but he seems to be on our side."

"Do not be deceived, Kingston One."

"Sepp is right," Geronimo agreed. "Beware of honey from a stranger."

"Anything new come up while we were gone?" Chris asked.

"*Ja.* We have learned, first, that Marak has been buying gold in large quantities for many months. We do not know what it is they want from TOAD."

"We seem to have two separate capers in progress," Chris said. "On the one hand, there are the Kronstein documents. TOAD may want them as international merchandise. It's certain that the Reds want them. That's logical, and Katabian and the Ace of Shadows make ample evidence. If they can't get the records themselves, they'll probably buy them from TOAD."

"Then there's the deal between Marak and TOAD," Geronimo said. "Whatever that is."

"But there's a hitch somewhere," Chris said. "Why does the action seem to center around

Kronstein Castle? Why was El Sidi there? Why are the Maraki agents there?"

"There's also the question of the gypsies," the Apache ruminated. "First the old woman warns us in Munich, then we get another warning from them all the way in Phrates. It doesn't make sense—unless someone with a pretty far-flung network is pulling the strings."

Chris contemplated this a while. "You might be on to something, Gerry."

"Great, but what is it? Do you think Jessica could be the puppeteer?"

Chris shrugged. "The Rom have a fantastically organized network of communication. There's hardly a corner of the earth over which they don't wander. And all along the way are a few trusted friends—such as Dietrich von Kronstein evidently was—and older persons no longer able to travel with the families or tribes."

"*Ja, ja,*" Sepp said. "I have heard this. These people act as contacts."

"Exactly. They're mail drops, telephone relays, and holders of information they've received by word of mouth."

"What about the old gypsy man living in Kronstein?" Geronimo asked.

"We should definitely talk to him," Chris replied. "I don't know how much we'll learn, though."

"Why?"

"Gypsies are notoriously devious. They've had to be, for their own protection," Chris explained. "Centuries of persecution made it necessary. Also, they're the most tight-lipped people in the world when it comes to talking about the Rom's affairs. A gypsy would rather have his hand cut off than to reveal a secret."

They were interrupted by a scratching from the rear of the shop. It came from the other side of the sliding panel used as a secret entrance to allow agents to enter and leave the shop unobserved if they wished.

Without a word, Sepp picked up a knife and began slicing a large piece of wurst. Geronimo and Chris hurried behind the blind side of a large refrigeration unit.

The scratching ceased. There was a *click* and the panel swung inward.

12 · Near-Miss

CHRIS AND GERONIMO fingered their anesthetic pens. Sepp was acting as bait. His back was to the secret panel and he pretended to be unaware of anybody else's presence.

A high-heeled shoe and a shapely, nylon-encased leg extended into the room. Then, stooping low, a pretty girl with red hair and green eyes entered.

"Spice!" Chris exclaimed. "What are you doing here?"

The TEEN agents stepped out of hiding as the redhead flashed a dazzling smile. "Hello, chums! I thought you were buddying it up with the premier in Marak."

"The premier decided he didn't want to be buddies any more," Chris explained. He turned to Sepp. "Sepp, this is Spice Carter, Vassar One."

"*Sehr erfreut*, Fräulein." Sepp clicked his heels together, bowed, and kissed Spice's hand.

"My pleasure, Herr Kalthuber. Your directions to the secret entrance were perfect."

Beaming, Sepp turned to the boys. "I knew they had arrived, but I had not the inestimable pleasure of meeting either of them."

Spice lowered her lashes demurely. "I wish all of our contacts were so charming."

"I hate to break into this lovely scene," Chris said. "But who's 'they'?"

Spice patted her hair. "My inestimably pleasurable self and Yummi Toyama. Berkeley Two. Without casting slur on your abilities, Q decided to send us in as a backup team."

"My heritage notwithstanding, I am not proud," Geronimo said. "On this case, we'll take help wherever we can get it."

"What's the drill?" Chris asked.

"Yummi and I have jobs at the Schloss. As maids."

"It is fitting," Geronimo said. "I have always tried to convince Q that the proper place for a woman is in the tepee."

"I love you too, Gerry. Anyway, today is my day off, and I came in to buy some skin-diving equipment."

The Kingston agents glanced at each other. "Skin-diving equipment?" Chris asked.

"Yes. I was swimming in Kronstein Lake the other day and I met a fellow who's a scuba enthusiast."

"What does he look like?" Chris demanded.

"Why, Kingston One! Are you questioning my taste?"

Geronimo answered. "No, just a concern that you don't end up permanently planted on the bottom of the lake."

The smile left Spice's lips. Chris explained what Geronimo meant. Spice said, "No, he doesn't look like either of the two you met. His name is Werner Haupt. He's twenty-four or twenty-five. Tall, deeply tanned, and handsome in the rugged, mountain man way. Besides, he might be of use to us later."

"I think we should check him out," Geronimo stated.

"Right," Chris agreed. "When are you meeting him, Spice?"

"Tomorrow after work."

The boys nodded. "Have you spotted anything at the Schloss yet?" Chris asked.

"There's an awful lot of searching going on. Lothar and that new servant Gunnar are tearing the place apart."

"Good. That means the records probably haven't been found yet," Chris said.

"Lothar isn't bearing up too well under the strain," Spice added. "He's growing more pale every day and seems to be getting thin."

"Someone might be putting pressure on him," Sepp suggested.

"That seems reasonable," Chris said.

"Yummi and I have picked up snatches of conversation between him and Gunnar. He said something about night prowlers and shadows making him nervous," Spice went on.

"The Ace of Shadows perhaps!" said Sepp.

"I think we should get that scuba gear now," Geronimo interrupted. "Outfits for three."

"I don't mind safety measures," Spice fumed, "but if you clowns bust up a good date, I'm going to clobber you."

"I believe the Fräulein is serious." Sepp chuckled.

"She is," Chris said.

Geronimo patted Spice on the head. "You're not to worry, little paleface. Your big brothers will be most delicate."

They said good-by to Sepp and left the wurst shop, after finding the address of a sporting-goods store in the telephone directory. On the way, they chatted about what they had been doing since they had last worked together. An article on the front page of a paper caught Chris's eye as they were passing a newsstand. "Wait a minute."

"What do you have?" Gerry asked.

"Our obituary."

Spice's green eyes widened. "What?"

Chris translated as he read:

" 'Two Americans Die in Crash. Associated Press Bulletin. Dateline, Phrates. Early this morning two unidentified young Americans crashed in a light plane. The accident occurred in the high mountains between Marak and Teleman, on the Marak side.

" 'The names of the victims are still unknown, but they are thought to have been students on holiday. A Marak official stated that the region is inaccessible by helicopter. The bodies will be brought down by volunteer climbers.

" 'Government planes investigated the site of the accident, the official said, and their reports indicate that neither of the youths could possibly have survived. He further stated that his government would notify next of kin as soon as the identity of the victims was known.' "

Geronimo grinned. "May I express my deepest regrets to you."

"And mine to you, Gerry."

"*What* is going on?" Spice demanded.

While they covered the remaining distance to the sports shop, the boys gave her the details of their trip. They finished the tale at the shop's door.

"You never pick the quiet assignments, do you?" Spice asked.

"Not if we can help it," Geronimo said, deadpan.

Inside, a clerk came up to them. "*Was wünschen Sie bitte?*"

They told him what they wanted, and he took them to a counter behind which were displayed fins, face masks, goggles, rebreathers, lead belt weights, depth indicators, waterproof watches, knives, spear guns, and related equipment.

A heavy-set, short, athletic-looking man entered the shop, looked about, then walked to the other end of the counter.

The TEEN agents were selecting simple, efficient equipment. The salesman said to the new arrival, "*Einen Moment, bitte.*"

"*Ja, ja,*" the man answered. He picked up a spear gun and turned it over in his hands, examining it with interest.

"If we can take three underwater watches along, I think that will be all," Chris said.

There was the snap of powerful rubber strips releasing.

Chunk!

"*Ai!*" The sharp head of a short metal spear creased Geronimo's cheek, then embedded itself deep into the wall.

The three TEEN agents whirled around. The short man was standing ten feet from them, spear gun in his hands. He was pale and looked stunned.

"You are hurt?" he stammered. "The gun . . . by itself . . . Oh! I am so sorry! Please!"

Geronimo stared at him icily and touched the stinging wound.

"Please, I am Peter Schlacht. Allow me to take you to my doctor."

"That won't be necessary," Geronimo said tonelessly. "You've done enough, thanks."

"I am dying with shame! There must be something . . ."

"Nothing."

"Forgive me. The embarrassment is overwhelming." Mumbling, "I am sorry . . . I am sorry," Schlacht backed out of the store.

Spice giggled with the release of tension. "It's a pretty poor Indian who gets shot with an arrow."

Geronimo grunted.

"I smell a rat," Chris murmured.

"A very large one," the Apache agreed. "And I'm going to find out where its hole is." He left to follow Schlacht. Chris and Spice remained to make the purchases and to retrieve the boys' car.

Geronimo emerged on the street and saw his

quarry rounding a corner. The Indian went after him. Schlacht made several turns, doubled back on his tracks, cut through half a dozen alleys, and behaved in general like a man who suspected he was being followed.

The song of the hunt was loud in the Apache's blood. He tracked Schlacht silently, invisibly, his eyes glittering, his lips pulled back in a wolfish grin.

At last, confident he could not have been trailed, the man slipped into an apartment building. Geronimo moved in after him.

Spice and Chris were waiting near the university in the Porsche, which had been repaired while the boys were in Marak. "It's been some time," Spice said. "You don't think he ran into any—"

Geronimo's voice crackled over their watch radios. "Tooey to Wunny." Chris acknowledged and Geronimo said, "Have package in hand. Come and see."

Chris made a note of the address and apartment number and gunned the Porsche away from the curb. Ten minutes later he and Spice were with Geronimo in Schlacht's apartment. The heavy-set man was unconscious at Geronimo's feet, a miniature transceiver in his hand.

"I thought we should make the call for him," Geronimo said sardonically.

A quick inspection revealed that the radio emitted an incoming-message beep when activated.

"Let's see who answers," Chris suggested. He switched it on.

There were several moments of silence, then a voice said, "*Ja?*"

"*Katabian?*" Chris asked.

"Fool! You shouldn't mention my—"

The radio went dead. "I guess that settles that," Chris said. "Another Red herring."

"Your friend Katabian got back in business awful fast," Spice said.

"He's in no hurry to leave Bavaria," Chris answered. "Probably located somewhere with a bird's-eye view of Kronstein Castle."

"We'll all have to be very careful," Spice said. "Don't forget that the slingshot champ got a good look at me in the scuba shop."

"You're an eyeful all right," Chris said, "but my guess is that Peter the Pious here only had eyes for Gerry." He gave Schlacht a nudge with his toe. The Red agent was still as cold as a mackerel.

They searched the apartment carefully. Spice found a pistol concealed in a small zippered pocket in Schlacht's brief case. It also included a few harmless papers indicative that their man was a wine salesman. But that was all.

"Leave his popgun here," Chris said. "We don't want to shatter his ego completely."

Spice wiped it clean of possible prints and replaced the weapon. "Now what? Shall we serve him to the cops on a silver platter?"

Geronimo shook his head. "No can do."

"He's right," Chris said. "We don't have a valid charge. And we couldn't prosecute anyway without blowing our cover."

"Okay, brain busters." Spice smiled demurely.

Chris drove Spice to her own car, waited fifteen minutes after she had left—so they wouldn't arrive together—then started with Geronimo for Kronstein Castle.

Lothar was outside talking to Gunnar when the youths' Porsche pulled into the driveway. His eyes widened and his jaw dropped.

"No!" he cried in a quavering voice. "More ghosts!"

13 · Flashing Hoofs

LEANING ON GUNNAR, Lothar fought hard to overcome his astoundment. He shook hands with the boys as if it were painful.

"Why did you call us ghosts?" Chris asked amiably.

"I . . . I had heard you were dead."

"Who told you that?"

"I—uh—don't remember. Someone said you had been killed in a plane crash."

"We're alive," Geronimo said. "Must have been someone else."

Lothar regained his composure. "Yes, obviously so. I was grieved when I heard, now I rejoice at your return."

"Thank you," Chris said.

"You will honor me by staying here again?"

"Well, we do have a few things to do, but we'd be pleased to spend what time we can."

After they had left the count, Geronimo said, "*Choonday*, things are not proper around the Schloss. Our names were not mentioned in the crash reports."

"And therefore whoever gave the word to Lothar has an inside line," Chris stated.

The TEEN agents arranged to meet Yummi and Spice in one of the castle's large bedding-and-linen closets the next morning, where they would be able to speak freely.

Spice looked on with an amused expression after introducing Yummi, a new addition to the TEEN network. The boys eyed the latest delight with obvious pleasure.

Yummi was a petite Japanese-American girl with almond eyes, a flawless golden complexion, and jet-black hair that reached nearly to her waist. She had a quick and facile mind and a coy little smile.

After a minute of teen-age repartee, Chris turned to business. "I'd like one of you to keep Lothar in sight at all times."

"Yes, master," Yummi answered.

Chris raised his eyebrows. "What?"

"Q said this was your case. We were to follow your orders absolutely. Like slaves."

Chris was embarrassed. "Q goes to extremes sometimes."

"Yes, master."

"Cut that out."

"Yes, master."

Chris flung up his hands in exasperation. Spice tried to repress a smile as Yummi said, "Seriously, chief, we'll—"

"Now you're poaching on my territory," Geronimo said.

Yummi bounced up on her toes and kissed the Apache lightly on the cheek. "Us minority types have to stick together."

The Indian looked confused, but pleased.

"Anyhow," Yummi went on, "you go do whatever it is that boy spies do. In the meantime, Spice and I will stick closer to the dear new count than the hairs on his head."

"Good. We'll check in later, after we've talked with the gypsy in the village."

"*Au revoir*," said Spice.

"*Ta-ta*," said Yummi.

Chris groaned. "Q," he muttered to Geronimo as the girls stepped quietly out of the closet, "has flipped, absolutely."

"Well, to each his own opinion, *choonday*."

The youths went outside to their car.

"To the old gypsy," Chris said as the wheels squealed on the cobblestones.

They drove to the village and found the address in the *Altstadt*, the old section. There they entered an ancient, yellowed building and climbed two flights of creaking stairs as Helga had directed them. Geronimo knocked. After a few moments the door was opened by an old, bent man with long, white hair. He had a deeply lined face and rheumy eyes, with which he regarded them suspiciously.

"We understand you might be able to tell us something about Count Dietrich von Kronstein and his friendship with the Rom," Chris said. "Something the Gaje don't know."

The old fellow hesitated, his eyes darting from one to the other.

"There *are* secrets," he said. "There are always secrets. But *tshatsimo Romano*."

Chris nodded. " 'The truth is spoken only in Rom.' "

The gypsy stared at the TEEN agent speculatively. "The Gaje do not often speak the tongue." He appeared to debate with himself, then went on, "There is an encampment of the Rom ten kilometers south of here. Go to them. Perhaps there you will find what you seek."

He closed the door. The boys heard the click of the lock.

"Not much to go on," Geronimo said.

"Maybe more than is apparent. At any rate, more than I expected. The Rom just don't like the Gaje."

They drove south from the village and found the gypsy camp in a field a short distance from the road, by the side of a small, winding river.

Chris parked and they surveyed a dozen wooden wagons painted with gay colors. Their doors were open, and protruding from narrow windows were large quilts and patchwork blankets airing in the sun. Wash hung from sagging lines strung between the wagons.

A few men with bright scarfs around their necks were repairing a broken wheel. Naked babies toddled about in the grass, and nearby colorfully dressed women were cooking over open fires in large iron kettles. A few horses were browsing in the shade of the trees, but several were in harness—a sign that the gypsies would be breaking camp soon.

When Chris and Geronimo stepped from their car, a pack of big, rangy dogs scampered from under the wagons and raced, barking, toward the boys. The TEEN agents stood still as the half-wild animals circled them, growling and yapping. A few gypsies looked up, but no one moved to help.

A knot of children appeared out of nowhere to watch the strangers' dilemma with amusement. Chris dug into his pocket and pulled out his miniature flashlight. He flicked it on and off. Desire spread over the children's faces.

Chris told them the flashlight was theirs if they would call the dogs off. There was a quick huddling of heads, then a slim boy stepped forward and shouted a single, harsh word.

The dogs slunk away. Chris handed over the flashlight. The slim boy snatched it and ran. His comrades pursued him noisily.

Chris and Geronimo walked to the center of the camp, where a couple of men were sitting on a log and eating stew from tin plates.

"*Droboy tume Romale,*" Chris said.

Nobody answered his greeting. An old woman appeared at the door of a wagon some twenty feet away. She pointed a bony finger at the TEEN agents and began screeching in Romany.

"What's she saying?" Geronimo asked.

"She's calling on the rest of them to throw us out of the camp. And she's laying curses on us. The most pleasant one calls for our hair and teeth to fall out, for our backs to be covered with boils, and for our tongues to shrivel in our mouths."

"That's the nicest one?"

"Yes."

"Don't bother translating the others."

Though he knew the gypsies disliked speaking to the Gaje in the Romany tongue, Chris tried again, because he realized he could trust what they said if they answered in Rom.

It was futile. He switched to German with the same result, then tried French. Finally he spoke to them in English.

One man ran out of patience. "Why do you bother us? The old count is dead. We loved him, but he is dead now. Go away."

Another man began to scratch himself violently. A woman emptying a pot nearby slopped some of the water over the boys' shoes. The old woman was still shouting.

"We are friends," Chris said. "We are trying to perform a service that was one of Count Dietrich's last wishes."

A dozen men and women clustered around the TEEN agents.

"Who was Count Dietrich? The Rom never knew him."

"Leave us. Go from here."

"I remember Count Dietrich. He is a fat little man in Austria."

"Count Deitrich von Kronstein hated the Rom."

"Just yesterday I was telling the count . . ."

Chris spoke to Geronimo in Apache. "This is what's known as The Treatment. Twenty different answers to the same question, scratching so you'll think they have lice, curses to scare you with."

A woman gave way to a violent coughing fit, as if she had tuberculosis. Another begged money from the boys.

Geronimo shook his head. "I'm afraid they've stopped us cold."

Chris nodded. He said to the gypsies in Rom, "I'm sorry you think us your enemies. I understand your distrust of the Gaje, but we were only trying to help."

He and Geronimo turned to go. The gypsies quieted, and smiled as they watched the strangers leave. A small child was crawling close to a team of horses harnessed to a wagon near the edge of the camp. Geronimo pointed. "Isn't that child too close to—"

A gust of wind swirled a piece of paper in front of the horses. They whinnied and reared. The child screamed.

Chris and Geronimo bolted forward. The horses' flailing hoofs were about to plunge down atop the baby. Geronimo threw himself in front of them. He waved his arms and shouted, *"Hai! Hai! Hai!"*

The animals remained on their hind legs, pawing the air. Chris dived, grabbed the child, and rolled to safety. Geronimo leaped aside at the same moment, and the horses came stamping down.

The camp was in an uproar. Gypsies were on their feet, shouting. Horses whickered and strained at their harnesses. Wagons were rolled forward, creaking.

The rescued child was still screaming as Chris

handed him over to a woman who came rushing up. In the babble of voices, Chris understood that this baby was somehow special.

A tall, thick-set mustachioed man clasped the TEEN agents strongly around the shoulders. "You risked your lives for a Romany infant," he said somberly. "You are welcome in our camp."

The atmosphere changed instantly. Women smiled prettily. Men shook the boys' hands. Someone brought out a violin, another a music box. Chris and Geronimo were led to a fire and offered a strong, highly seasoned, delicious broth and steaming mugs of coffee. A long-legged, beautiful gypsy girl began a spirited dance, her thick petticoats flashing.

The boys were feasted and entertained most of the afternoon—but their hosts still refused to discuss Count Dietrich. When it came time to leave, a dark, long-haired young man in heavy black boots accompanied Chris and Geronimo to their car.

He said, "Concerning what you heard in The Treatment: there are lies more believable than the truth. Remember that."

"I do not understand what you mean," Chris said.

"Understanding takes time." The gypsy slipped a scrap of paper into Chris's hand. "Read this when you have returned to the Schloss."

Respecting the gypsy's wishes, the boys did

not look at the paper until they were back in their room. Chris unfolded it, frowned, then passed it to Geronimo.

"Nothing but an address in East Berlin," the Indian said. "How are—?"

He was interrupted by a warning beep, then a message that came over both their watch radios.

"Berkeley Two to Kingston One and Two. Come in, please."

Chris answered Yummi's call.

"I'm worried," the girl said. "Vassar One went skin diving with her friend after she finished work. She was going to check in with me, but I haven't heard from her, and I haven't been able to raise her on radio."

"Understood," Chris replied. "Where did she go?"

"Felsenriff. It's opposite Kronstein, the deepest part of the lake."

"We're on our way. Over and out."

14 · Three Seconds to Live

THE VILLAGE OF Felsenriff sat on the north end
of Kronstein Lake. Stretching west of Felsenriff
was a mile and a half of coves, bluffs, and small
cliffs overlooking the deep water. Chris and
Geronimo pulled into the brush at the start of
this rocky coastline and concealed their car.

They walked along the road quickly, checking
parking spots until they found a red Saab at a
public wayside. Three stony paths led down to
the water.

"Haupt's car, probably," said Chris.

"Wait a minute, *choonday*." Geronimo pointed
into the woods where a small patch of white was
scarcely visible. "They're not alone."

The boys went into the forest and tore the

branches away from a concealed white Volvo with a dented left rear. They recognized the car instantly—the skin divers'!

Geronimo silently raised the hood and removed the distributor cap. He hid it in the brush. Returning to the wayside, the TEEN agents determined that two of the paths led directly to the rocky beach below and that the third approached by a circuitous route. They chose the last to avoid detection.

Chris broke the silence as they were descending. "Looks as if we were right about Werner. He's in with them."

Geronimo nodded. They crept to the beach but saw nothing on the quiet water. "They must still be down," Chris said. "It's a question now of whether we wait, or get into our own gear and go after them."

"The question's been answered." Geronimo pointed to a spot some thirty feet offshore, where lines of bubbles were boiling the surface.

The youths drew back and found cover. Two divers broke water. Each was shepherding a rubber-suited figure who appeared unable to move by himself.

Spice Carter and Werner Haupt!

As the quartet gained the shore it became obvious that the TEEN agent and her date were bound tightly with thongs. The mysterious divers dragged their captives roughly.

"Now?" Geronimo whispered.

"Only if it looks necessary. Maybe we can learn something by waiting."

One of the thugs drew a rubber-handled underwater knife from its sheath on his thigh. He approached Spice. Chris leveled his anesthetic pen, thumb resting lightly on the firing clip.

"All right, sweetheart," the goon said. "I'm going to cut you loose and then you're going to answer a few questions. Don't try anything funny."

When Spice's bonds were cut, she stood up and rubbed her arms and legs. Glaring at her abductors, she removed her bathing cap, shook out her red hair, and fluffed it. "Are you quite ready?" she asked.

"What do you mean?" the goon with the knife said.

"This!" A savate kick caught the man's wrist and sent his weapon spinning into the water. He bellowed and rushed the girl. His companion closed in from the other side. Spice whirled. Her hands stiffened, her arms swung, stabbed, and for a few moments she was a blur of wild motion.

When it was over, her assailants were lying stunned and groaning at her feet.

Chris applauded. He and Geronimo rose into view. Spice shot them an angry look. "How long have you two been here? Least you could do is give a girl a hand."

"You hardly seemed to need one."

The three of them untied Werner. "What happened?" Chris asked.

"We were diving a couple of hundred yards out. Then we saw these two jokers beneath us. They spotted us at the same time and waved us off."

"I thought they had a fish," Werner explained, "and did not want us to frighten it. I was willing to go, but not Fräulein Carter."

"I didn't like the way they acted," Spice went on. "They came closer and made angry gestures. I did the same to them. They got the drop on us with spear guns and forced us to the bottom. They tied us and held us there until our oxygen was nearly out." Spice patted her hair. "The brutes."

"I'd say you paid them back double," Geronimo remarked.

Spice smiled. "Why do you think they didn't want us around?"

"Treasure!" Werner said excitedly. "They must have located an old Nazi treasure cache. There are several that have never been found."

"Possible," Chris said dubiously. "We'll let the Felsenriff police find out, if they can. Gerry and I will tie these two and stop at the station on the way back to the Schloss."

"It occurs to me," Geronimo said, "that we haven't been introduced yet."

"Oh, I'm sorry." Spice presented Geronimo and Chris to Werner. "I'm so unhappy our date turned out this way, Werner. I was having such a good time."

Werner drew himself up. "It was educational, Fräulein Carter," he said stiffly. "I did not know you were so proficient in martial arts."

Spice smiled. "Well . . . that . . ."

"Explanations are not necessary. But perhaps it would be better if I find a date who does not make me feel so inadequate."

Chris chuckled. "I must admit you weren't really at your most delicate and ladylike."

Werner was marching up the hill. Spice dashed after him. "Werner, please wait! We can talk about this!"

"Ugh, romance," Geronimo grunted.

Chris and Geronimo trussed up the divers. Then, after notifying Sepp and the police, the boys headed back to the castle. While Geronimo went to make sure Spice had returned safely, Chris wandered out into the darkness of the small park to study the topiary work again.

There in the moonlight stood the shadowed sculpture that resembled the Ace of Shadows. Now, if someone with a light were—

His reverie was shattered by two figures which hurtled out of the blackness. They struck the

TEEN agent simultaneously and bowled him over. A canvas hood was dropped over Chris's head and pulled chokingly tight around his throat with a drawstring.

Blinded, his chopping hands could not find vital spots on the attacker. His wrists were seized, shoved hard behind his back, and handcuffed.

The men worked in silence. They hauled Chris roughly to his feet and shoved him forward. Then each of them seized an arm and half dragged, half carried him.

Chris heard the sound of squeaking hinges. He stumbled over a step and went to his knees. Then he was bulldogged up a spiraling flight of stone stairs. He realized his abductors were taking him to the top of the castle tower.

The TEEN agent tried to keep his cool. But he was nearly suffocating and his pulse thumped like a jackhammer.

The men finally thrust Chris into a chair and roped him tightly. He heard one of them leave.

"Now, old chap," said the remaining man in thick Oxford English, "we are going to chat. Tell me, please, are you a Maraki agent or a Red agent?"

"I'm a student at—"

His inquisitor rocked Chris's head. "Do not attempt prevarication! Only the truth is acceptable."

Chris breathed deeply. "I am a student at the University of Munich."

"Oh, bother! This is simply too wearisome for words. Save your breath, Mr. Cool. It really matters very little whether you work for the Communists or the Marakis. In either case you must be eliminated. Do not feel discriminated against, though. Your frightful Indian friend will join you in the grave shortly."

Chris heard the unmistakable sound of a revolver being cocked. He steeled himself against the impact of the bullet.

"*Unh*." Thud.

Beneath the hood, Chris frowned. The sounds made no sense to him. "Are you going to shoot, or not?"

"If he does," answered a female voice, "no one is going to be more surprised than me. That sleepy sliver should keep him out for more than an hour."

"Yummi!"

"Humbly at your service, master." She loosened the drawstring and plucked the hood from Chris's head.

"How in the world did you get here?"

Yummi was fishing in the pockets of Chris's unconscious tormentor for the key to the handcuffs.

"Simple." She rolled the man over.

Gunnar!

"I told you I'd stick to Lothar. I watched

him and Gunnar grab you. Our good count is at the bottom of the stairs now, sleeping off a sleepy sliver himself."

"Yummi, I love you!"

"Thank you. I have always thought myself a lovable little girl."

She found the key, freed Chris, and went down the stairs with him. She patted Lothar on the head as they stepped over him. "Sleep tight."

They met Geronimo and Spice in the Schloss, scouring the rooms looking for Chris and Yummi.

"We've got to work fast," Chris told Geronimo. "It's obvious we can't do any more good around here. I think we should beeline for East Berlin."

"Right. What about Yummi and Spice?"

"Lothar and Gunnar have no idea what hit them. They'll suppose it was you. The girls' cover is still good, so they might as well stay."

The boys grabbed their bags, which were still packed, climbed into the Porsche and were on their way. While Chris drove, Geronimo radioed Sepp. He told him what had happened and where they were going.

Sepp instructed them to stay at the Hotel Oser. Their contact would get in touch with them there and arrange for a student tour into East Berlin.

Chris and Geronimo drove on through the night, heading north to Berlin. At daylight they checked into their hotel, where a package was waiting for them with specially tailored suits. They took the package to their room and then collapsed with exhaustion into their beds. Their alarm was set to ring at one o'clock.

At two-thirty they handed their papers to the American soldiers on duty at Checkpoint Charlie. With them in the car were Andreas, their East Berlin chauffeur, and Kurt, a CIA man in the guise of their West Berlin chauffeur.

The crossing gate was lifted and Kurt drove the limousine into the No-Man's Land that separates East from West Berlin.

At that instant a burst of machine-gun fire split the air.

15 · Karl Marx Street

THE TEEN AGENTS and the two Germans stiffened. The machine gun clattered on.

"There!" Kurt said, and jerked the wheel of the limousine hard to the right.

East German police were firing at a car headed away from the Communist side of Checkpoint Charlie. The car slewed violently and came to a stop.

The driver staggered out, hands clasped to his bleeding forehead. East German police swarmed about the car, brandishing pistols.

Kurt edged the limousine forward and passed the stricken vehicle. The trunk was riddled with bullet holes and two men in uniform were trying to pry it open with a crowbar.

"A refugee in the trunk," Kurt said coldly to Andreas. "Your police are rather drastic in their methods."

Andreas shrugged. "A man who breaks the law is a criminal. Nothing more need be said."

As visiting students, it would have been impolite for Geronimo and Chris to have criticized their "hosts" for the day. But both boys had to exercise tremendous effort of will to remain silent.

They were passed into the Communist sector without problem. The border guards seemed ill at ease over the shooting and wished to move witnesses on as quickly as possible.

Now that they were in East Berlin, Andreas took over the wheel and began the tour of the "old city." In a boring monotone the Red chauffeur launched into a formal lecture.

"In the beginning of the thirteenth century," he said, "the locality of Kölln arose on the island in the Spree, and Berlin was born on the right bank of the Spree. Both places are mentioned in records dating back to A.D. 1237, when the metropolis made its first appearance on the scene of history.

"In 1432 Kölln and Berlin merged into one city. In 1470 the castle at 'Kölln an der Spree' became the permanent residence of . . ."

Andreas droned on. He was an official guide of the East Berlin government and his English was quite good. Years of experience with tourists, however, had blunted his enthusiasm and he plowed through his monologues with all the emotional excitement of a computer.

Chris and Geronimo finally could stand no more. They interrupted Andreas, begging him to set aside his prerecorded speeches and give them an off-the-cuff tour. At first the driver seemed quite upset. He was unaccustomed to dealing with situations not described in his training manuals.

But when Chris and Geronimo continued to pressure him, Andreas relented.

Now the TEEN agents began to enjoy themselves. Andreas realized that nothing catastrophic was going to happen and gradually thawed. He even smiled as he chatted with the Americans.

Driving slowly, their guide passed the burned-out remains of the Chancellery. Later, they stood in somber silence in the bunker Hitler had occupied during the last hours of the war, when Berlin was being destroyed around him, and in which he took his own life.

They visited the once-beautiful Deutsche Oper Berlin, and from there, crossed Unter den Linden to view the memorial to the Communist Unknown Soldier.

The boys were pleased to see that visitors could take photographs freely. After the incident at Checkpoint Charlie, they had feared that East Berlin would have all the oppressive earmarks of a police state.

"They certainly put on a good show for the tourists," Chris whispered.

A sense of well-being and camaraderie had been generated in Andreas. He confided that, "Even though the wall divides us in two, we do not think of East Berlin and West Berlin. There is only Berlin! And we are *all* her citizens."

Chris, Geronimo, and even Kurt, smiled. Whereupon their driver, perhaps thinking he had gone too far, said gruffly, "Of course there would be no wall if it were not for the capitalist warmongers. Someday all peoples and all nations will enjoy the peace and blessings of Communism."

"Sure thing," Geronimo spoke up. "But in the meantime your border guards still find it necessary to shoot people who want to desert to the 'decadent' West."

Andreas looked embarrassed. "Well . . . well . . ." He raised his hands in a gesture of bewilderment.

Chris quickly changed the subject and Andreas looked relieved.

In a short, whispered conversation in Apache, the agents agreed that they had spent enough time in the role of tourists to blunt the suspicions of anyone who might have been watching them. They asked Andreas if it would be possible to see Karl Marx's old dwelling place. Their East Berlin address was quite near it.

"*Ja*," he said, pleased. "I would be most happy to show you."

A short drive brought them to the site. The house was a small and undistinguished one—part of a long row. It would never have been singled out were it not for the plaque set into its brown facade. The boys got out of the car and crossed the street. They read the plaque, then stepped back to get a fuller view of the place.

At the same time, they were studying the street. It was empty except for a man and woman strolling arm and arm down the sidewalk. The TEEN agents waited until the couple had passed them and turned the corner at the intersection. There was no traffic.

Chris and Geronimo sauntered back to the car. In the back seat the Apache raised his eyebrows.

Chris nodded.

"Well," said Andreas, "how did you like—?"

The anesthetic pen in Geronimo's hand went *phhht!* The chauffeur slumped unconscious over the wheel.

Kurt moved fast. He scrambled out of the car, walked around the front, and entered the driver's door. He removed Andreas's cap and put it on his own head, then unclipped the East Berliner's guide badge and fastened it to his own lapel.

Kurt checked for passers-by. Nobody! He eased the Communist across the seat, pushed him down into the space under the dashboard, and covered him with a blanket. "All set, boys."

"Nicely done, Kurt," Chris said. "Find us a nearby alley where we can change without being observed."

Kurt turned over the engine, put the car in gear, and pulled away from the curb. He found a deserted alley three blocks away and stopped.

Chris and Geronimo stripped off their suit coats and pants, turned them inside out, then put them on again.

Kurt nodded approval. The TEEN agents now wore suits with muted colors, wide lapels, and a slightly unkempt look. From their pockets they took wide neckties and peaked caps of the type worn by German students. The square-toed German shoes they wore completed their disguise.

"Excellent!" Kurt said. "You are perfect East Berliners. My congratulations."

"Our best wishes to your technical staff," Chris said. "They did a bang-up job on such short notice."

Kurt acknowledged the compliment with a little inclination of his head. The trio synchronized their watches.

"Andreas will be out for about an hour," Chris said. "We'll meet in front of the Karl Marx house at six-fifteen."

The boys left the car and walked out of the alley. Four blocks later they turned left.

"Oh-oh," Chris said. "We goofed. This should be the street but it isn't."

They paused, undecided. "We can't very well take out a map," Geronimo said. "We'd hardly look like natives."

"Agreed. Well, it can't be far off. Let's retrace our steps."

They turned and went back the way they had come. Geronimo said, "If we— *Iltse!* The local fuzz is headed our way."

An East Berlin policeman was walking directly toward them. "*Halt!*"

The pair stopped. "*Ja?*" Chris said.

The policeman asked what they were doing. Chris told him they were searching for his professor's house. The policeman wanted to know where the professor lived. Chris gave the man the right street, but a fictitious address.

The officer looked them over, then evidently decided he was being ridiculous. He smiled and told the boys how to find the street.

"*Danke,*" Chris said. "*Guten Tag.*"

"*Bitte.*"

"Man," Geronimo breathed when they were

out of the policeman's earshot. "Remind me to never distract you when you're doing language homework again!"

Chris chuckled.

They found the number—a nondescript rooming house, and stopped before it.

"If anything goes wrong," Chris said, "the police will be looking for two men. I think we should split up and meet later."

"Then you go in," Geronimo said. "Your German is perfect."

It was decided that while Chris went inside, Geronimo would drift, and be ready either to escape quickly or to come to Chris's aid if summoned by watch radio.

Chris waited until the Indian was out of sight, then he went up the steps and knocked on the door.

An elderly woman with a cane answered.

Chris said, *"Die Zigeuner Von Kronstein haben mich geschickt."*

The woman gasped, motioned him in quickly, and locked the door. She chewed her lower lip while she looked him over. Then she made her decision and beckoned him to follow.

The woman led the way down a long ramp into a subbasement. She knocked in code upon a storage-room door and whispered, "A man is here. He says the gypsies of Kronstein sent him."

With that she backed away. The door swung open. Chris gasped, dumbfounded.

Before him stood a spare elderly man, dressed in a green silk robe with matching cravat which set off a thin aristocratic face. He had iron-gray hair, brushed back neatly, a large hook-nose and deep-set pale blue eyes, which looked directly at the TEEN agent.

The man bowed slightly and extended a large hand. Chris grasped it and nearly winced at the pressure.

"*Dietrich von Kronstein,*" his host said quietly.

16 · Where Is Geronimo?

SLOWLY, AS IF in a dream, Chris released the iron handshake.

His brain was whirling. The man who stood before him was a carbon copy of the person he had seen in the coffin! A twin? Plastic surgery? What was the answer? Who would go to all this trouble? And why?

"You are an American, yes?" The question was in English.

Chris nodded.

"Good. If you have gotten this far, then you must be an agent of your government. And a trustworthy one. Otherwise the Rom would have done away with you long before you neared this place."

Chris was reluctant to admit his official status.

But he reasoned that his cover was pretty much useless now, and he decided to gamble in the hope of winning additional information. "Yes, I'm an agent."

"Good. We are being honest with each other. Sit down, please."

Chris took the chair the count indicated. Von Kronstein drew up another chair. Chris kept himself poised, ready to spring into action at any threatening move.

"Your Central Intelligence Agency is very efficient," the count said. "But there are some things they cannot discover by themselves."

"Such as?"

"The key to your present mission."

"We're working on it."

"You are still wary of me, *ja?*"

"As a friend of mine might say, I'm just scouting the terrain. After all, I did attend your funeral."

Von Kronstein chuckled. "Indeed. Well, I will tell you this. Return to Schloss Kronstein. Go to the tower room. Examine the third block of granite that faces north."

"What will I find?"

"That, my young friend, you will discover soon enough. But you will be well pleased, I assure you."

Chris studied the count silently.

"Something confuses you?"

Chris could not help smiling. "I'd say that's a pretty fair summation."

"Well, do not be disturbed. I have discovered that the older one grows, the more complex and bewildering life becomes. Only the very young and the very foolish believe differently."

Chris relaxed a little. "I'm young and a little bewildered, too. My friend and I received a warning in Munich—from an old gypsy woman. Minutes later she was murdered."

Von Kronstein nodded. "Yes. A very old friend. I felt her loss deeply."

"Then you were behind the warning?"

"I did not say that."

"But you don't deny it."

Von Kronstein was silent.

"Later, in Marak," Chris went on, "we were contacted by another gypsy."

"The Rom cover the entire earth," the count said.

"Your work again?"

"Perhaps. Perhaps not. All life is speculation of one form or another. Little can be known for certain."

"Count von Kronstein, what can you tell me about a man known as the Ace of Shadows?"

"The Ace of Shadows? I know nothing. If we conjecture, though . . . The Ace is always the highest, *ja?* Or the most. A shadow—what is a shadow? A falsity. Something that appears to have substance, but that does not. A shadow is nothing, really. So the Ace of Shadows would be the most of nothing. Something that does not exist, eh?"

As Chris probed for a clue to that remark, the count rose, bowed slightly. "Time passes and I grow tired. I have enjoyed your company, but I am afraid I must now bring this interview to a close."

He showed Chris to the door. The elderly woman was waiting outside to guide the TEEN agent back upstairs.

"Remember," Von Kronstein said, "the third granite block."

"Facing north," Chris answered.

"*Ja.*" The count shook hands. "Good-by, my friend. Good luck."

The woman led Chris out of the basement up to the landing. She opened the door for him and held it. She had not spoken.

"*Danke schön,*" Chris said. "*Auf Wiedersehen.*"

"*Auf Wiedersehen.*" She closed the door behind him.

Outside, Chris glanced at his watch. It was ten minutes to the time he was to meet Kurt and Geronimo in front of the Karl Marx house. He walked slowly in that direction, hands jammed deep in his pockets, forehead furrowed.

If the man he had just met *was* an impostor, then why had he told Chris about the stone? A booby trap? Possibly, but Chris didn't think so. It was too chancy and elaborate; there were simpler ways to remove thorns from your side.

And there was the matter of the gypsies. *They* had given him Von Kronstein's address. Chris felt dead sure the gypsies were loyal to no one but themselves and the old count.

But why had the man been so evasive about the Ace of Shadows? Surely there was no reason for him to withhold information about a Red agent.

Most important, if this man was the real Count Dietrich von Kronstein, then who had been buried in the family mausoleum?

Chris reached the rendezvous point five minutes early. Neither Geronimo nor the limousine was there. He strolled around the block, consuming three minutes, and when he returned he saw Kurt pulling up to the curb.

He slid into the back seat and changed his clothes. Both agents glanced up and down the street. Geronimo had not appeared.

"By my watch," Kurt said, "Andreas will be regaining consciousness any minute now."

Kurt hoisted Andreas up from the floor, propped him behind the wheel, and replaced his cap and guide badge. "If your friend does not return, we are in serious trouble. We cannot afford to keep Andreas asleep for another hour."

Chris nodded. "Set the watches back. If Gerry

doesn't show, we'll knock Andreas out again and try to get across the wall alone."

The CIA man turned Andreas's watch exactly one hour back. Then he and Chris made similar adjustments on their timepieces.

"Not much longer to go," Kurt said.

Chris's lips were pressed into a thin line. *Come on, Gerry, come on!* he thought.

They had to leave. The mission demanded it. But how could he abandon his pal?

"We're in trouble," Kurt said nervously.

Andreas groaned. His eyelids began to flutter.

Chris grimly clenched his jaw and readied his anesthetic pen.

"Let's go!" Kurt said.

Chris's finger hesitated over the firing clip.

There was the sound of pounding feet. Chris jerked around to see Geronimo streaking toward the car. The Indian came to a skidding halt, yanked open the door, and leaped inside. Out of breath, he gasped in Apache, "Joined a . . . Communist tour group . . . got swept up in . . . their propaganda . . . forgot time." He changed his disguise swiftly.

Andreas was shaking his head. He rubbed his knuckles into his eyes, then stretched and yawned.

Chris went into his act. "It's really thrilling to see the actual house," he said. "Reading about a man or a place in a textbook just isn't the same."

Suddenly Andreas glanced about, a perplexed look in his eyes. "That is odd," he said in a slurred voice.

"What is?" Chris asked.

"I feel . . . I feel as if I have been . . . dreaming."

"A daydream perhaps?" Kurt asked.

Andreas looked at his watch. It assured him that only moments had passed since their arrival at the Marx house "Yes. It must have been a daydream."

"Well," said Chris, "I imagine it gets a bit boring, showing the same sights month after month."

"No, not at all. Please do not think I have been bored. It is a service I am happy to perform for my country."

Chris said this was the last site they had planned on seeing, and considering that they had a dinner engagement in West Berlin, they should probably head back to Checkpoint Charlie.

Andreas started the car. They had driven only a few blocks when Chris saw a clock tower two intersections ahead. He nudged Geronimo.

The limousine neared the tower. The large clock face became visible. Andreas looked toward it.

Suddenly Geronimo shrieked and flung himself hard against the door.

"Driver, stop! Quick!" Chris cried out. "He's having a fit!"

17 · The Cemetery's Secret

ANDREAS WHEELED OVER to the side and slammed on the brakes. Geronimo's timing had been perfect. The driver had not seen the clock.

The Indian writhed in the back seat, choking and coughing. His eyes were squeezed shut. Hands and feet flailed about wildly.

"What is it?" Andreas asked.

"I don't know," Chris said, putting a note of hysteria in his voice. "I've never seen anything like this happen to him before!"

"Give him first aid," the Communist said.

"*How?*" Chris wailed forlornly.

Andreas said to Kurt in German, "The boy's too frightened to help his friend. Why don't you climb into the back seat and assist him?"

"I know nothing of first aid," Kurt replied.

Andreas muttered something insulting about West Berliners.

"Please!" Chris said. "He's going to die!"

"Be calm. It will be all right." Andreas turned to Kurt. "I will administer to the lad. You drive the car. Two blocks ahead you will come to Friedrichstrasse. Turn left and you will be headed directly toward the checkpoint."

Andreas got into the back and Kurt slid behind the wheel. The CIA man lost no time pulling back into traffic.

Kneeling beside Geronimo, Andreas said, "First we check to make sure he has not swallowed his tongue." He pried open the Indian's mouth and peered in. "Good. Now we loosen his tie and open his collar button."

"I'll do it," Chris said hurriedly. He had to make sure the East Berliner did not spot the gimmicked suit.

"That is correct," Andreas observed pedantically. "Now you take one of his hands and I will take the other. Rub them vigorously. We want the blood to circulate."

"Is he going to be all right?"

"Yes, I believe so. You see? He is growing calmer already."

From the corner of his eye, Chris saw Checkpoint Charlie. "What a relief. I was worried."

A few moments later Geronimo's eyelids

opened. He groaned, looked around with surprise, and said, "What happened?"

"You were overexcited, perhaps tired," Andreas said, "and you had a small seizure."

Kurt pulled the car up beside the East German guardhouse.

"How do you feel?" Chris asked.

"A little weak, but I think I'm all right."

"Would you like me to call a physician?" Andreas asked.

"No, thank you. It's not necessary."

"Well, then I will say *Auf Wiedersehen*." He shook hands with the boys. "I hope you enjoyed your visit."

"Immensely," Chris assured him. "We learned quite a bit."

When Andreas stepped from the car, East German police made a quick, thorough search. They checked the trunk, examined the underside, lifted out the seats. Satisfied there were no hidden escapees, they allowed the car to pass through.

As soon as they were safely in the western zone, Chris, Geronimo, and Kurt let out a long, collective sigh of relief.

"Very inventive, Mr. Johnson," Kurt said. He turned to Chris. "Was your mission a success?"

The TEEN agent answered with a nod.

Kurt dropped them off at their hotel. The boys quickly checked out, left West Berlin, and drove straight to Munich for a consultation with Sepp.

On the way, the Apache was brought up to date on the mysterious Dietrich von Kronstein.

It was well after midnight when they entered the sausage shop through the secret door in the rear. They had radioed Sepp a few miles out of Munich and so he was awake and waiting for them—with a full pot of fresh coffee and thick, very welcome sandwiches of spiced meat and musky cheese.

While eating, they discussed what they had learned in East Berlin.

"I think the man I met is the legitimate Count Dietrich von Kronstein," Chris said. "It all fits— the gypsies, the information he gave me, his intelligence, his manner."

Sepp pulled at his ear. "I am inclined to agree. But if so, then we are left with a corpse whose identity is not known."

"Two wampum belts to one says it's a wax dummy," Geronimo said.

Chris shook his head. "No takers."

"In any event, we must know for certain," Sepp said.

"Next stop the Kronstein Cemetery," Geronimo said.

"But after some sleep," Chris added. "I don't think we could walk a dozen steps without falling on our faces."

"*Choonday*, you speak with very straight tongue."

"There are cots in the room behind the refrigeration unit," Sepp said. "Sleep as long as you wish. There is no hurry."

The boys brought their suitcases into the spare room and dug out their pajamas.

Sepp appeared at the door. "One more thing. I sent one of our men to oversee the interrogation of those skin divers you captured."

"It was Spice Carter who caught them," Chris said.

Sepp raised his eyebrows. "So? Our man said they were quite battered. This Fräulein Carter is not to be taken lightly."

Geronimo laughed. "That's what her date thought, too."

"Unfortunately," Sepp continued, "neither of the two could be persuaded to talk. They are most stubborn. They insist they grew angry merely because their fishing was interrupted."

Chris sighed. "Too bad. But if we can't strike pay dirt with the count's information, we can always backtrack and follow up the underwater angle."

"Just so. Now good night, my friends. Sleep well."

The TEEN agents awakened about three in the afternoon. They had breakfast of rolls and coffee, then went to the Deutsches Museum and wandered a few hours through the rooms of scientific displays, the U-Boat, and the simulated mines in the lower level.

Toward dusk they stopped for a light dinner, and as darkness began to slide down the mountain slopes, the young agents drove to the village of Kronstein.

"Are you ready, my dear ghoul?" Chris said as oncoming car lights flashed past them.

"Apache gravedigger scared. Suppose we meet Dr. Frankenstein?"

At the west end of the village, a cobbled road twisted and climbed up a hill to the cemetery at the top.

Since their car would have attracted undue attention moving up the winding road to the graveyard, the boys pulled into a back alley, left the Porsche, and made their way through the darkened cobblestone streets on foot.

"*Choonday*," Geronimo whispered suddenly, "we're being followed."

Both boys whirled. A shadow ducked behind a tavern. Immediately the boys took evasive tactics. They stepped into a restaurant and left by the kitchen door, much to the surprise of the portly chef. Geronimo led the way down one alley and up another, over a five-foot stone wall, through a flower garden, across a small apple orchard.

Fifteen minutes later Chris said, "I think we've lost our shadow."

Geronimo agreed, and they began making their way to the cemetery again. They reached the stone pillars and the unlocked iron gates at the hill's crest. The crypts, headstones, and small monuments were hardly visible on either side of the tree-lined lane that wound through the cemetery.

As Chris reached for the gate, a low baying filled the night. Three figures were moving quickly up the slope.

Chris recognized the silhouettes. "Katabian, Schlacht, and their monster! Inside, hurry."

The TEEN agents sprinted into the cemetery. Kronstein was not a large village, but it had buried many inhabitants over the centuries and the graveyard was wide and sprawling. The boys ran broken-field style, but the hound kept on their trail, its baying moving ever closer.

"*Koya!* This way!" Chris said. "Behind that big monument!" They ran past the giant stone angel and ducked behind it.

"No sleepy slivers," Chris said. "I want to ask these goons a few questions."

Geronimo ripped off his tie and fashioned it into a noose as Katabian and Schlacht came racing up, close on the heels of the bounding dog.

The trio streaked by the monument. "Now!" Chris shouted.

He and Geronimo sprang out. Chris brought Katabian down with a tackle around the waist. Geronimo backhanded Schlacht to the ground, then turned to meet the dog. The beast went up in the air, fangs bared, straining for the Indian's throat. Geronimo ducked. The dog overshot and wheeled for another rush.

The Apache was poised on the balls of his feet. The hound snarled and leaped. Geronimo side-stepped agilely, slipped the noose over the dog's muzzle, and pulled it tight. Both went down in a tumble.

Pinning the beast with his knees, Geronimo yanked the end of the tie behind its head, then knotted it to the other side of the noose. The dog's mouth was clamped shut.

Chris had dazed Katabian, then turned to face Schlacht, who had recovered from Geronimo's blow. Schlacht dropped into a knife fighter's crouch, a keen blade in his hand held with the cutting edge up. Horrid guttural sounds came from his throat.

Chris tempted him with an arm. Schlacht took the bait and slashed. Chris jerked his arm back and caught Schlacht in the kidney with a karate kick. The German grunted, dropping his guard. Chris lanced forward and spilled the man with a palm blow to the center of the forehead.

Katabian, sitting on the ground, was shaking

his head. "All right," Chris said. "The party's over. Now we want to know—"

With a lightning motion, Katabian jerked something from his pocket and hurled it to the ground. It *plopped*, and immediately a green mist spread, rising rapidly. Chris and Geronimo started to choke.

"Get away!" Chris gasped.

There was no time to use the nostril gas filters. The TEEN agents staggered out of the mist, eyes streaming, throats burning. They stood coughing for several moments. When they had recovered, they inserted nose plugs and went back into the green cloud. Katabian, Schlacht, and the dog were gone.

"Think they're coming back?" Chris asked.

Geronimo already had his flashlight beamed on the ground. "I'll track 'em." The footprints, visible only to the Apache, led to the cemetery gate.

"I guess that's that," Chris said.

They made their way finally toward the crypt that housed the remains of the Von Kronstein family. The mausoleum, looming dark and ominous, was massive, squat, and unadorned. Chris went to work on the lock with a thin plastic sheet and a jeweler's tool. It clicked open.

Geronimo remained outside to stand guard. Chris entered the cold, dank tomb, and using his light, found Count Dietrich von Kronstein's coffin. The bronze lid was locked. "That's funny," Chris muttered. He laid his light on a nearby stone coffin and picked the lock.

One-two-three! He hefted the lid, reached for his flash, and played the light over the count's familiar features.

He touched the face. It was rubber—a mask!

His excitement mounting, Chris found the nearly invisible seam in a fold of the neck. He gripped the bottom of the mask, clenched his teeth, and ripped it off.

A startled cry tore from his throat.

"Jessica Valorsky!"

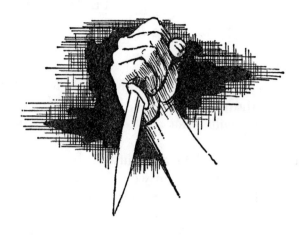

18 · Dead Man's String

GERONIMO CAME RUSHING in. "What's the drill, *choonday?*"

"Take a look." Chris centered the light beam on the corpse's face.

"Wow!"

The young woman was in her twenties and pretty. Her black hair was cut short and her oval face had a somewhat pixieish look about it.

"We've finally found Jessica," Chris said. "No wonder we smelled her perfume in the chapel." Chris lowered the lid and snapped the lock.

"This seems to clinch it," Geronimo said. "You were right. The man you met must be the real Count Dietrich von Kronstein."

"But what's he doing in East Berlin?" Chris mused.

"Vacationing?"

At this, Chris shot his buddy a sour glance. Geronimo shrugged and said, "He can't be there against his will. After all, the gypsies knew how to find him."

"And I walked in and out scot-free."

"Dietrich said our answer's in the tower. You believe him?" Geronimo said.

"There's one very excellent way to find out."

They left the mausoleum, locked its door, and started back down the hill to the village. While they walked, Chris contacted Spice and Yummi by watch radio.

"Vassar One and Berkeley Two here," Spice answered. "Go ahead, date-wrecker."

"Troubles with Werner?" Chris asked.

"How could there be? He won't come within a hundred feet of me."

"Sorry, but it really wasn't our fault, you know." Spice growled.

"How are things going at the Schloss?"

"Routinely," Spice said. "Situation unchanged since you left."

"All right. Gerry and I are on to something that may blow this case wide open." He told her about Jessica Valorsky and Count Dietrich. "We have to come to the Schloss, to the tower, to be precise. But we can't chance it while Lothar,

Gunnar, and who knows how many of his other playmates are around."

"So you want notice as soon as the coast is clear, right?"

"A-plus."

"Okay. We'll keep a tight watch. If it looks as if it's going to take too long, Yummi and I will see what we can do toward setting up a diversion."

"Good girl. That's it."

They reached the village and approached their car indirectly, to surprise anyone who might be watching. They saw no one.

Chris drove a few kilometers out of Kronstein, then pulled off the road into the woods. They could not chance being seen, so they planned to sleep in the Porsche. They flipped a coin for the first watch. The job fell to Chris.

While Geronimo was working himself into a comfortable position, Chris uncapped his snooperscope for a quick scan of their surroundings.

He moved the scope in a circle and had almost completed the check when he stiffened. "Gerry, we've got company."

A wavering, partially blocked red outline had appeared in the lens.

Geronimo's anesthetic pen was in his hand and he was reaching for the door. "Many?"

"No, just . . . Oh, for crying out loud!"

"What?"

The image had taken on definition—four slender legs, a graceful arched neck, and a rack of antlers.

"It's a deer," Chris said. "Sorry."

"It is obvious, paleface chum, that your ancestors were not woods dwellers. Night."

Chris read for a while, using the thin beam of Geronimo's flashlight. But as the hours dragged by, his consciousness was dulled by the stillness of the night. He snapped himself alert several times. Gradually, though, he lost the sense of the book and the words began to blur into each other. The moon was well past its zenith when his head dropped to his chest and the book slipped from his hand. . . .

The TEEN agents woke with a start. Both were looking into the muzzles of black automatics.

"Resign yourselves," said a voice. "There is *no* way out this time."

Half obscured by the swirling mist of dawn, Chris saw the two gunmen, obviously Marakis. With them were four henchmen dressed in camouflage suits.

"What do you want?" Chris asked coldly.

"Information."

Two of the camouflaged men opened the doors. "You may get out," said their leader. "I trust your intelligence will prevent you from trying anything foolish."

Chris and Geronimo slid out of the car and

stood with their feet spread and their arms folded across their chests.

"Good. Now . . . where is Jessica Valorsky?" the Maraki asked.

"We haven't the faintest idea," Chris answered.

The Maraki sighed. "I am not going to waste time. Stating the matter simply, we intend to torture you until you speak. And you will speak. You are both clever enough to know that tortures of the Eastern world will loosen any man's tongue."

"What's the deal if we do tell you?" Chris asked.

"No deal. But you will save yourselves some rather excruciating pain."

Faint sounds of hoofs and creaking wagons and tinkling bells drifted in from the road—a gypsy caravan on the move.

"Well . . ." Chris appeared to weigh the situation. "All right. You'll find Jessica Valorsky in the mausoleum of the Von Kronstein family."

The Maraki raised his eyebrows. "What is she doing there?"

"She's dead."

"You killed her?"

"No."

"Who did?"

"I don't know. We found her, that's all."

The Maraki turned to the Apache. "Your friend speaks the truth?"

"Yes, though you might find that concept hard to understand."

The Maraki sneered. "You Americans! Always so noble. What does nobility get you? Nothing. Nobility is for fools!"

"We'll keep that in mind," Chris said.

The Maraki smiled thinly. "It is doubtful you will keep anything in mind very long." He motioned to a pair of his henchmen.

They drew thin silken cords from beneath their jackets and stepped forward.

"What's this?" Chris said.

The sound of the gypsy caravan was drawing closer and he was stalling for time.

"Please. You are experienced enough to recognize garroting cords."

"But we told you where to find Jessica Valorsky."

"And you escaped torture. But you cannot escape death! Be honored that the method of your execution has such an ancient tradition."

"One request!" Chris said as the thugs moved in for the kill. "Let me leave a message for my mother. With the gypsies." He jerked his head toward the road.

The Maraki deliberated. "All right. But I warn you that I read English fluently."

Chris asked Geronimo for a pencil and paper.

He whispered in Apache, "The Dead Man's String too."

Geronimo pressed the string into Chris's hand when he gave him the writing implements. Chris palmed the string. Under the watchful eye of the Maraki leader he scribbled:

> *Dearest Mother,*
> *I will never come back, but do not mourn for me. I am happy.*
>
> > *Love,*
> > *Chris*

"Give it here!" The Maraki snatched the note and studied it carefully. Then he started to laugh.

"What's so funny?" Chris asked.

"You think the gypsies are good postmen. That they will mail your letter, eh? Ha! They are thieves!"

"You promised my last request."

"All right. On with it."

Chris scribbled an address on the back of the letter, then pulled a ten-mark note from his pocket.

The six Marakis walked with the TEEN agents to the side of the road. Chris flagged down the lead wagon by waving the ten marks. A tall gypsy eyed them suspiciously, handed the reins to his wife, and jumped down.

Behind Chris, the Maraki had hidden his gun in his coat pocket. Chris met the gypsy halfway. He extended the note and asked if the man would post it in the next town. When the gypsy nodded and reached for it, Chris dropped the Dead Man's String into his hand. Chris said in Romany, "Sweet dead one, let the noose about to be tied around my neck be undone."

The gypsy's eyes widened. He looked back to the waiting caravan, shouted an order, then yanked a long knife from the sheath on his belt.

19 · Blowup

LONG-HAIRED GYPSY men in bright shirts and leather boots leaped from their wagons. Sharp knives in their hands glistened in the early-morning sun. Within seconds the gypsies had surrounded Chris, Geronimo, and their captors.

The Maraki leader's gun was leveled at Chris's head. "I'll kill you!" he ranted.

"Don't be stupid, Gajo," said the tall gypsy. "We will cut you into little pieces and feed you to our dogs."

The Maraki's finger quavered on the trigger.

"And the cutting," the gypsy continued, "will take a long time. A very long time."

The Maraki dropped his gun. Before it could touch the ground Geronimo snatched the weapon, unloaded the bullets, and dropped it into his pocket.

Chris and the gypsy leader spoke for a few moments in Romany. When the conversation ended, the tall man addressed the Marakis. "Our young brother asks us to let you go, so we bow to his wishes." He sheathed his knife with a flourish.

The Marakis glared at the TEEN agents. "We will kill you for this," their spokesman said. "Remember that. You are condemned men!"

"Go!" snarled the gypsy. "Run like the curs that you are, or we will finish this the way I want to!"

The Marakis needed no further prompting. They whirled and fled into the woods.

Chris explained to their perplexed rescuers why he insisted upon freeing the Marakis. "They'll head right to a certain cemetery," he said, "and when they find the body of a certain lady agent, all Helvetia will break loose."

Geronimo's mouth set in a tight grin. "The Marakis, Reds, and TOAD will play ring-around-the-coffin."

"Ha, you know white man's game." Chris chuckled.

The gypsies urged Chris and Geronimo to remain with them a while for their own protection. The TEEN agents agreed, especially since the next step was to await word from the castle.

The boys were given tribal clothes—neck scarfs and flamboyant shirts, loose-fitting pants and handsome boots. Their Porsche was driven up a plank ramp into one of the larger wagons and the doors were closed behind it.

The caravan leader invited the boys to ride with him in the lead wagon. He waved, snapped the reins across the horses' backs, and the caravan rolled forward.

At midday the wagons pulled into a field beside the road. Cooking fires were lit, kettles slung over them. Lunch was being dished into the boys' plates when their radios crackled:

"Vassar One to Wunny and Tooey Kingston. Come in, please."

Chris answered.

"Big doings here," Spice said. "Jessica Valorsky's body has been found. The whole town's in an uproar. Lothar's been called down to the cemetery. Most of his men have gone with him—all except friendly Gunnar."

"So we can hit the tower?"

"Like straight arrows."

"Good. We're on our way."

The boys unlimbered their Porsche, declined the gypsies' offer to help, and headed for Schloss Kronstein.

When they roared through the gates, a figure leaped out of the brush. Chris jammed on the brakes.

"Greetings," Spice said. "Thought I'd keep watch here and pick up advance notice on any of the returning natives."

"Good idea. Everything still serene at the battlements?"

"Like a sleeping baby."

"Good. Yummi?"

"She's waiting for you."

"Check. Keep posted and let us know by radio if anybody shows."

"Will do."

The Porsche sped away with a spray of gravel. Yummi met them at the castle door.

"So happy to see most venerable masters," she said. "You've come to present us with all the answers?"

Chris patted her on the head. "In time, little one. In time."

"Where's Gunnar?" Geronimo asked.

"Went stalking to his room a minute ago with a face that would make a Gorgon look beautiful."

"Let's eavesdrop."

The three agents climbed the stairs, then walked softly down the hall to Gunnar's room. Chris pressed his ear to the closed door. Gunnar was speaking.

"Yes, sir . . . Yes, sir," he said. . . . "No, we don't know who killed her yet. Either the Reds or the Americans. . . . No, no word on the count. We still don't know where he is. . . . Yes. . . .

The last gold deposit? It's to be sunk late this afternoon. . . . Right. We'll clear out after that."

There was a long period of silence, then Gunnar's "over and out" indicated he had been talking on radio. The TEEN agents moved quickly away from his door and went back down to the ground floor.

Chris told Geronimo and Yummi what he had heard. "So," he said, "it looks as if Jessica was the go-between for TOAD and the Marakis. The Reds seem just as interested in this mysterious deal as we are."

"And it'll probably be wrapped up by tonight," Geronimo said. "That doesn't give us much time."

"Speaking of time," Yummi said, "we're wasting it by standing here."

"Righto. Let's go!" Chris opened the door.

They went to the tower and climbed the long flight of winding stairs to the summit.

"Here are the blocks of granite," Chris said.

They quickly examined the third one. It appeared identical to all the others.

Yummi said, "You've been fooled, Wunny."

"Wait!" Geronimo passed his fingertips over the masonry at the base of the stone block. Peering closely, he made out a hairline circle. The Apache put his thumb against it and pushed.

The granite block swung inward.

Geronimo peered into the blackness. "It's a secret passage with another flight of stairs."

"Good Indian!" Yummi exclaimed.

"Let's take a look," Chris said. "Yummi, you stay here and keep watch." Chris pondered a moment. "And as a second precaution . . ."

He and Geronimo removed the adhesive strips of explosives from behind their ears and fixed them to the passageway's entrance. Then, with flashlights in hand, they went down the dark and damp-smelling stairs.

Moisture dripped from the walls and the flashlights revealed great, glistening spider webs.

The stairs ended in a pool of greenish water. Filtered light was visible at the bottom. "So that's the bit," Chris said. "An underwater exit that leads to the lake."

"*Gonzone*," Geronimo said. "But it's still not what we want. Unless the records are hidden here somewhere."

"Berkeley Two here," came Yummi's urgent voice over the radio. "I hope you cats have a way out down there."

"Affirmative," Geronimo answered. "Why?"

"Lothar, Gunnar, and two more bullyboys are hotfooting it up the stairs, carrying very ugly machine guns."

"They must have slipped past Spice."

"At the moment, master, that is irrelevant. I'm on my way down."

Seconds later the boys heard Yummi's foot-

steps, then a powerful white light illuminated
the passageway, framing Yummi like a quiver-
ing moth.

"Stop!" Lothar demanded. "All three of you!
Stay where you are, or we'll cut you to ribbons!"

"The booby traps," Chris whispered.

The boys flipped open their ruby rings, ex-
posing the detonating devices. Yummi was three-
quarters of the way down the stairs. Lothar and
his crew had just begun to descend.

"I think Yummi's out of the blast area," Chris
whispered. "We'll have to risk it. Another ten seconds and those goons will have us."

Chris shouted, *"Down, Yummi!"* Then he and
Geronimo clicked their ring mechanisms into firing position.

The top of the tower blossomed into orange
flame, then disappeared as the explosion rever-
berated in the stairwell. Pieces of stone clattered down and dust billowed everywhere.

The boys played their flashlights into the haze.
A vague form appeared.

"Yummi!" Geronimo cried. She stumbled into
his arms, frightened.

"You cats play awfully rough," she said.

"But not quite rough enough," came Lothar's
voice.

He was leaning against the wall, face blackened
with grime, forehead gashed and bleeding. A

Russian burp gun was cradled in his arms, its snout covering the TEEN agents.

Suddenly a single shot came from behind the Americans. The burp gun flew from Lothar's hand!

Chris whirled to see a man step from a niche in the wall, a pistol in his hand. He wore a flat, wide-brimmed hat. His face was masked by the high collar of his long cloak.

Chris gasped.

"The Ace of Shadows!"

20 · Ace in the Hole

"THE SAME," SAID the Ace with a bow. "Count Dietrich was not the only one to know of this secret passageway. Or the place in which these were hidden." He held up an aluminum microfilm capsule. "The records," he said quietly. "On microfilm."

"You found them!" Lothar cried. "Excellent, excellent. Now you'll give me the promised money and the deal will be complete."

"Hardly."

"Is this a double cross?" Lothar demanded.

"In a manner of speaking." The Ace threw off his hat and slipped out of his cloak. He was a handsome man, whose features bore a marked resemblance to Lothar and Count Dietrich.

Lothar's face turned ashen under the soot. "Hasso!" he screamed.

The Ace looked at him icily. "Yes, dear brother."

Chris and Gerry exchanged startled glances. "I understood that you had been drowned several years ago."

"A story of convenience, Mr. Cool."

"You know our names?"

"Certainly."

Geronimo snorted. "While your father's been helping people escape to the West, you've been hunting them down!"

With lightning speed, Hasso took a cigarette lighter from his pocket and pointed it at Lothar, who collapsed.

"Now there. . . . To answer your charge, Mr. Johnson. You are wrong. Here!"

The Ace tossed the sealed capsule to Geronimo. As the Apache's hand flashed up and caught it, a puzzled look flickered across his face.

The Ace gave a small smile. "I know who you work for, and I'm sure you'll take proper care of these records."

"I don't understand," said Chris.

"I have been a double agent from the beginning. My father and I were able to work more effectively that way."

Geronimo bit his lip. Then his piercing eyes looked straight into the Ace's. "I am sorry, sir," he said. "I spoke too soon."

"It is understandable," replied the Ace. "Now I must ask your aid. I was sent here with Katabian and Schlacht, who were shadowing me, on a twofold mission. First, to prevent a deal between TOAD and Marak. TOAD needs gold to pay their scientists, who are currently developing nuclear arms. In exchange for the gold, they have agreed to sell nuclear potential to Marak."

Chris whistled. "And the Communists don't want Marak to possess atomic weapons any more than we do, right?"

"Correct. Such power in the hands of an irresponsible government can have terrifying results. Katabian shot El Sidi in an attempt to stall the transaction. I am afraid, though, that we are no closer to success than in the beginning."

"Perhaps we have the answer," Chris said. He told the Ace about the skin divers off Felsenriff and about Gunnar's radio conversation.

"Clever," Hasso said. "You *have* solved that riddle, I'm certain."

"Geronimo and I will see it through," Chris promised.

The Ace nodded. "Thank you."

"What was the second part of your mission?" Chris queried.

"To buy the records, naturally, which I would report as an impossibility. TOAD, ironically, tried to get in on that deal. Jessica Valorsky bid for

them to sell them later at a profit. My father
scorned her."

"Who killed her?"

"My brother takes credit for that, Mr. Cool.
Jessica got to him with her offer. He imprisoned
my father in the tower and tortured him in a
vain effort to learn where the records were hidden.
He even faked father's death to gain control of
the Schloss and the family estate."

The TEEN agents looked incredulous as the
Ace went on. "Our family fortune had shrunk to
almost nothing and Lothar needed money badly.
Jessica refused to take No for an answer from
Lothar and tried to blackmail him into giving up
the records. She knew his tower secret. He was,
as you say, in a bind. So he killed her. Then he
had a mask fashioned and prepared an elaborate
funeral."

"While Count Dietrich was held in the tower?"

"Yes."

"How did your father escape?" Geronimo
asked.

"There was always a gypsy watching from the
shadow topiary for the count's messages. One
of them picked up his distress signal. I broke
into the tower, released Father, and took him to
East Berlin where he continued his work for
humanity. It is the most effective cover of his
whole career. We planned to let Lothar stew in

his own juice until after the Marak issue was settled. That had priority."

"Why didn't you get the capsule before?" Geronimo asked.

"Katabian and Schlacht were keeping too close a tail on me. So I instructed the gypsies to guide you to Father. It was his decision to let you get the records yourself."

"Then why are you here?"

"You two have been having your troubles—" Geronimo and Chris grinned.

"So I thought you might be too late. I was wrong."

"One more question," Chris said. "How does Gunnar figure in all this?"

"Lothar needed a gunman in case of trouble. He did not realize he had hired himself another TOAD agent."

Hasso turned to his brother. His glance revealed the deep contempt he felt.

"*Choonday*," Geronimo said abruptly, "if we want to intercept that gold delivery we'd better be on our way."

Without a further word, Hasso von Kronstein shook hands with the TEEN agents and bowed slightly to Yummi. Then they parted.

Taking the only way out, the three TEEN agents plunged into the greenish pool, swam toward the light, passed beneath a stone ledge, and broke the surface on the other side. A few people were running excitedly in and out of the castle, with hardly a glance at the trio.

Once ashore, Yummi was dispatched to Munich with the capsule of microfilm. Then Chris radioed to Spice. She was on the stairway to the tower, helping police pick through the rubble. Hearing the buzz on her wrist, she retreated to a secluded spot and replied.

"Oh, Chris, I was so worried! Are you all okay?"

"Fine. Just wet. We found the Ace!"

"You *what?*"

"Don't get excited. Now here's what we'll do to raise that cache of gold." After a brief explanation he signed off.

Chris and Geronimo stepped from a taxi onto Broadway near Fifty-sixth Street in Manhattan. They peered into the showroom of Luxury Motors, which was filled with a variety of expensive foreign sports cars.

Inside, Chris approached a salesman. "I left my Jaguar here for repairs. Is it ready yet?"

"You'll have to speak to the manager, sir. Right through that door, please."

The boys went into an anteroom. A pretty blond secretary pressed a button. Chris and Geronimo walked through another door into an elevator. Chris spoke into an intercom grille:

"Kingston One and Two for debriefing."

They shot to the top floor, where a guard scrutinized them through a port of bulletproof glass, then triggered the door open.

The TEEN agents walked down a carpeted corridor, past the steel-doored code room and the top-secret Special Projects laboratory. They stopped at a flush-paneled door at the end of the hall. An electronic eye scanned them, a green light flashed, and the door opened.

"You are precisely forty-five seconds late!" Q barked. He was bent over his massive walnut desk with its built-in monitor screen. An unlighted pipe jutted from his grayish-blond beard. A half-empty bottle of milk, which he used to soothe his ulcer, stood within easy reach.

Yummi and Spice were standing in front of the desk.

"Well," Q growled, "how was Bavaria?"

Chris and Geronimo recounted their mission.

Q gradually lost his scowl as he listened to the report. "So," Chris finished, "the gold was towed to the police dock and turned over to the West German authorities. Lothar and his henchmen were taken into custody as well as Katabian and Schlacht."

"Gunnar talked," Geronimo said. "Helped us round up some Marakis and a few TOAD agents. Then we went directly to Munich, booked a flight, and arrived at Kennedy this morning."

"Nice job, chaps. You, too, dear ladies." From Q that was the *highest* praise. "However, you haven't cleared up all the loose ends, I'm afraid." Q reached for his milk bottle and swigged. A little milk clung to his mustache, which he neatly wiped with a handy paper napkin.

"Such as?" Chris queried.

"That man Schlacht? Why did he try to kill you, Geronimo?"

"He didn't, sir. That was a bungling accident. Schlacht was eavesdropping."

"Just fiddling with the spear gun, sir," Chris added.

"And the helicopter? Who dropped the flare on you?"

"Katabian and Schlacht," Chris replied. "They tailed us to the woods and radioed for the copter."

Q leaned back and pressed his palms together. Chris anticipated the TEEN boss. "Sir, if you'll pardon me, I think I can answer the question you were about to ask."

The chief eyed him. "Carry on."

"You want to know how Lothar thought we were dead."

"I found out," Yummi said brightly. "TOAD's network picked up the story and fed it to Gunnar. He told Lothar."

Q did not bat an eye. His fingertips still touched.

"Something else, sir?" Geronimo asked.

"Of course," Chris said. "What about the Kronstein ghost? Isn't that it, sir?"

Q nodded almost imperceptibly.

Chris explained that after Hasso had found his father, Count Dietrich was hidden in the town for a few days while arrangements were made for smuggling him into East Berlin. "But several old folks glimpsed him," Chris said. "Hence the ghost. I believe that covers everything, sir," he added.

"Mm, seems so," said Q. "I suppose you know it was the Ace who had you warned in Munich and Marak. Heads a big network of gypsies, I understand."

"Where is the Ace now?" Chris inquired.

"Nobody ever knows but the Ace . . . and his gypsy wife. And his little son—whom you saved from the horses by the way."

"The Ace's kid?" Chris whistled. Geronimo shook his head slowly.

"Quite."

"Pardon, sir, but I have a question."

"Yes?"

"That coded list of names we discovered—what were they?"

"They? Oh yes. Very clever. Decoded too late to help you. That was a list of the gold shipments already sunk in the lake."

Spice spoke up. "Where is Count Dietrich?"

"Back home in Bavaria. He invited all four of you to spend a quiet vacation at Kronstein Castle next year. TEEN will pay the expenses."

"Thank you, sir!" Chris and Geronimo said.

"You're a dear," Spice purred.

Yummi bent over to kiss him.

Q turned scarlet. "Out! Out!" he blustered. "This very second—or I take it back!"

"Yes, sir!" Grinning, the four TEEN agents hurried through the door.

GERONIMO
JOHNSON